ENDING EDEN

THE PENDING FATE OF HUMANITY

MICHAELANDRE MCCOY

Outskirts Press, Inc.
http://www.outskirtspress.com

Paperback ISBN: 978-1-9772-0840-8
Hardback ISBN: 978-1-9772-0841-5

This book is dedicated to my wife, Virginia,

whose love and encouragement have been inspirational.

TABLE OF CONTENTS

PROLOGUE

I'm supposed to tell you that this is a work of fiction. I'm not supposed to tell you that it is a secret transcript made from a recording I believe was recently forwarded to me on behalf of a very special being from the stars that I met many years ago. Those close to me know just how much that first encounter has changed me forever.

Whether the following transcript is real or not, I'll let you draw your own conclusions; but I have personally researched the existence and histories of the places and people cited in this transcript and found them all to be valid. I would strongly encourage you to also extensively research the **bold**, highlighted references on the Internet.

As a courtesy, I have also included pictures and paintings, taken from the Internet, of many of the subjects referred to within.

The *italicized words* are translated "thought projections" also recorded on site by Their advanced Celestial technology.

I realized early on that I could not, in this book, solely do justice to the numerous accounts, references, and documented information to be found on the thousands of reference sites on the web and on television shows such as *Ancient Aliens*.

This transcript should be used as an informative guide to the innumerable undeniable facts that all lead to one plausible, and I believe, insurmountable conclusion.

The **Antitruth** surrounding mankind's origins and "assisted development" is well documented, but remains disassociated like the disassembled pieces of a gigantic picture puzzle scattered all over the world.

The truth is indeed out there, if we would only choose to see and acknowledge it.

Otherwise, take from this what you will; but if what I have learned from these transcripts is true, our world will change dramatically in the near future, with the pending fate of humanity hanging in the balance. How? Why? You'll have to read to understand.

CHAPTER 1

ANONYMOUS INTRODUCTIONS

Australia: Peru has finally arrived. Let Us begin.

Washington: *Let us begin by pointing out the total disregard and disdain for others exhibited once again by Ms. Peru and her uncanny propensity to keep others waiting.*

Peru: *Can I help it if I have been forced to take a commercial flight while my perfectly good private jet awaits me at the airport? Besides, I'm an hour and a half earlier than I was the last time, so I'm getting better.*

Australia: We all arrived on commercial flights under assumed names. I have already explained to you at length about the need for heightened security, and you assured me that you understood.

Peru: *Just because I understand doesn't mean that I agree with your protocols, or like them. You know how I detest flying first class amongst the unwashed masses.*

Ethiopia: *That doesn't seem to deter you from drinking their Starbucks coffee. I can't believe you made a stop on your way here, when you knew that we were holding up the Council meeting until you arrived.*

Russia: *You didn't expect her to drink this dishwater the hotel calls coffee, did you?*

Japan: *I take offense to that! This is one of the finest hotels my holding company has in its portfolio. Must I remind you that you are staying here free of charge.*

China: *Yes, free of charge because our host refuses to let us use our credit cards or cell phones… "for security reasons."*

Rome: *My credit cards and cell phone were also confiscated. I feel almost naked without them.*

Israel: *I can't believe those two thugs at the door had the nerve to frisk me. I've killed men for less!*

Australia: Those "thugs", as you call Them, are Pures just like the twelve of Us. And We're all aware that you are a Mossad agent, so there is no need to constantly remind Us. We all possess exemplary stature within our respected countries. If We didn't, We wouldn't be here.

India, what are you doing?

India: *Meditating and levitating. Oh yes, and admiring Peru's beautiful necklace.*

Peru: *Why thank you, Ms. India. You are obviously the product of good breeding and refined taste...unlike some of the others in attendance. This was a last-minute departure gift from my wonderful husband, to remind me that no other man on this God-forsaken planet will treat me better than he does.*

Ethiopia: *No other man is brave enough or foolish enough to try!*

Peru: *I see you're still stinging from your last attempt to court me ten years ago.*

Ethiopia: *Woman, if I had wanted you ten years ago you'd be mine by now! This is something you can believe! You should be so lucky.*

Peru: *And you should see a psychiatrist!*

Egypt: *Ms. Peru, why would you blame any man for desiring your company? He'd be insane not to.*

Peru: *You've got a point.*

Australia: Okay, let Us put an end to this before We put an end to each other. Britain, I have noticed that you have remained silent through all of this.

Britain: *I seldom join children when they are at play. I prefer to observe and codify.*

Russia: *Observe and codify? What is that supposed to mean? Must I remind you that all of us here have Royal Pure blood? You are no more special than the rest of us, and I will not tolerate being looked down upon by some snooty English witch!*

Britain: *That's an "Irish Traditional Witch", if you don't mind. In the future get your facts straight before making a fool of yourself. Witchcraft is based upon the ancient technologies and pharmaceutical practices handed down by my ancestors.*

Careful that I don't put a hex on you, old man!

Russia: *Old man! I'll show you who is an old man!*

What the hell...I cannot rise!

Australia: *That would be my doing.*

Russia: *But that is impossible. No man can mentally restrain me. I have been taught by the masters. Was it something in the coffee? I knew it! Peru was wise not to trust you!*

Peru: *Don't drag me into this.*

Russia: *Are the rest of you just going to sit there and let him get away with this unwarranted attack on my dignity? I am no man's prisoner!*

Australia: You may rise now, if you still desire. I was just making a point.

Russia: *I am going to make it a point to smash your face in! Who do you think you are?*

Australia: I am the Chairman of this Council. And as long as I am, no one will be smashing anyone's face in. Now sit down!

I SAID SIT DOWN !

Russia: *My god, he isn't human. He can't be. No man can control me like this!*

Australia: *You are correct. No ordinary man can, but I have been fitted with certain "enhancements" to ensure the safety of everyone in attendance. I can override any attempted mental blocks, detect any attempt to lie or to mislead, and disable any or all of you with a single thought. But let us all hope that it doesn't come to that.*

Now, unfortunately, I must insist that everyone in attendance cease to "thought-speak" and begin speaking out loud in English. These proceedings are being recorded by the secure transcorder device you see at the center of the table. Although it is capable of recording thought projections, I will be adjusting it so as not to inadvertently record any thoughts you may wish to keep private.

Rome: Why English? Why not Italian or Spanish?

Australia: Because English is the only common language We all speak outside of Our own. And some of Us, who shall remain nameless, still lack proficiency in the language of Our ancestors.

Russia: I bet it's the witch.

Britain: *Shhuu...tahhh!*

Russia: Did you all hear that! No one speaks to me that way and lives. Mr. Chairman, I must insist...

Australia: You threw the first punch, Russia.

India: Yes, and I, for one, must insist on civility during these proceedings.

— 5 —

Australia: And I, for one, must insist that you stop levitating and lower yourself back into your seat.

China: Yeah…show-off!

India: Do I detect a note of jealousy in your tone, my friend?

China: We haven't been friends for ten years, so let's not pretend now.

India: Civility.

Japan, Rome, Egypt and Ethiopia: Civility!

Washington: I can't take any more of this supercilious dross… I'm leaving.

Australia: I think not. No one is leaving these proceedings until they have concluded. It has been brought to my attention that We have a spy among Us. And until We ferret out who it is, no one leaves, and everyone is under suspicion.

Russia: My vote goes for the guy with the enhancements and a false sense of superiority.

Egypt: I agree. Who died and made you Chairman?

Australia: Apparently, it was your predecessor from Saudi Arabia.

Since this Council last convened ten years ago, he has been found guilty of treason and taken off-planet for re-patriotism counseling.

Japan: I heard that he fathered three children with a Mute.

China: Some of Us find that term offensive.

Washington: What would you rather We call them… "Dims"?

China: Of course not, but must We speak of our mentally challenged brethren in such derogatory terms?

Rome: I, for one, have no problem with using the term. I've called them much worse. China, you don't have any Mute children, do you?

China: Of course not! How dare you ask me a question like that…*gro-bahhh*!

Britain, Japan, Peru and Egypt: Civility!

Australia: Civility indeed. I haven't heard that word in thirty-plus years.

Israel: Yeah, there's a reason for that…it was once punishable by death.

Britain: Oh come now, that's an old wives' tale.

Russia: You would know! And what's with that stupid cape?

Australia, Japan, Ethiopia and Peru: Civility!

India: If Britain doesn't stop glaring at Russia that way, I'm going to move to the other side of the room. It's not healthy to allow oneself to be continually bombarded with so much negative Karma. I have felt a headache coming on since I got here, and it is becoming almost unbearable.

Egypt: You too! I thought it was just me.

Japan: You're not alone. The psychic aura in this room is poisonous. Let Us please seek out some semblance of decorum and return to the agenda at hand.

Britain: Hear, hear!

Washington: I think it's Mr. Enhancements over there that's causing the problem.

Australia: I assure you that my enhancements have been thoroughly tested and critiqued ad nauseam. It's not me, but I have been scanning the room to try to locate the source.

             I have eliminated the possibility that one of Us is less than a Pure by allowing you all to telepathically communicate. And although I have uncovered some potentially damaging secrets that some of you are attempting to block me from discovering, they are all of a personal nature and thus shall remain undisclosed.

             Before you say anything, remember that any protest shall be met with distrust on the part of your fellow Council members.

Washington: Well, I've got nothing to hide, outside of my growing hatred of Mutes.

All: Civility!

Japan: In light of that last remark I would like to lodge a formal protest as to the continued participation of Mr. Washington. He is clearly not open-minded.

Washington: And you are clearly a Mute lover.

Japan: I must insist on civility, Mr. Chairman. Either you rein him in or I will!

Washington:	I'd like to see you try, "Rice Man". I'd really..............
Australia:	Would you like to see *me* try, Mr. Washington? If you're through insulting Mr. Japan, I'll allow you to breathe again.
	I will take your nod as acquiescence.
	Council members, fellow Pures...are We not better than this?
Washington:	Where...can...I...get...some of those enhancements?
Egypt:	Perhaps We should vote on electing a new Chairman who does not need to lead via intimidation. If you do that to me, I will never rest until I make you pay for it.
Australia:	And you will end up a drooling, brain-damaged, wheelchair-riding vegetable.
	Maybe We should begin anew with some proper introductions.
	The guidelines are that no one discloses their real name or the actual city in which you reside. As I said, there is a spy among Us.
	This was brought to my attention when a confidential source of mine, who is working under cover with the "Free Earth Movement", which is determined to bring an end to this **Anunnaki** Council, was contacted by someone in this room.
	No one else, including our spouses, were supposed to know where or when this Summit would take place.
	That is why I must insist that you, Mr. Washington, surrender your other two cell phones, and you, Mr. Japan, turn in the iPhone in your coat pocket.
	Anyone else want to avoid embarrassment?
	Thank you, Ms. India. They will all be returned to you at the end of the Summit.
Washington:	But what if one of my children...never mind.
Australia:	This Anunnaki Council has been meeting for over two thousand years. One or two of you even have forefathers who attended past Summits. Long ago, Summits were held every one hundred years, but for the past fifty years We have begun meeting on a ten-year basis due to Earthkind's sudden rapid advancements.

For those of you who may be unaware of the Council's history,
the **Anunnaki,**

reportedly from the planet **Niburu**, were but **one of several** organized Celestial Pure groups who sought to bring enlightenment to Earth Humans many thousands of years ago, from several different star systems.

Let me correct something. Niburu is most definitely NOT on a 3,600-year orbit around our sun. Physics dictates that the "planet" would freeze solid for thousands of years, which would extinguish all life on the planet. The same would've occurred if Niburu had ever collided with another planet.

Now, Earth Humans, primarily the **Sumerians, Assyrians, Akkadians**, and **Babylonians**, who sometimes called Them the **Igigi,** considered the Anunnaki gods, or deities. The Igigi, however, are a working-class sect of Anunnaki who built many of the original Pure Colonies here on Earth, within which They themselves once dwelled. The name Anunnaki means of royal blood, or as We would say today, They were Celestial Pures.

Earth Humans were led to believe that today's **Modern Man** is supposedly the end result of genetically modified cavemen created by the Anunnaki to be slave labor. This misinformation persists even to this day.

As We are all well aware, Non-pures, or Mutes as some would call them, were relocated here, in relatively small groups from *different* planets, at multiple sites on every habitable continent on Earth, by Overseers from their respective ancestral planets Who spoke their dialects and shared their disparate customs. They were to be freed from the slavery our common ancestors had subjected them to, due to their mental deficiencies; i.e., their inability to use telepathy, telekinesis, or to levitate; and their diminished capacity to store and recall information.

Thousands of years later, many Overseers determined that the Earth Human population numbers had grown sufficiently large enough to effectuate the construction of large edifices and complex stone cities with the advanced technological tools They had brought with Them. Others also used Mutes to mine precious minerals and ores from beneath the earth's surface.

By this time, none of the original "Drops" or "Firsts", as some like to refer to them, were still alive. Only a verbal history of Earthkind's arrival and development had survived, and most of that history had subsequently been clouded by mythos, superstition, conjecture, and purposeful manipulation.

The Anunnaki and others seized upon this confusion and, for the most part, convinced some Earth Humans that They, the Anunnaki, were in fact **Creation Deities** that should be both incontestably obeyed and feared.

In defense of the Ancient Overseers, Earth Humans showed few signs of developing along any significantly cohesive path without Their help and guidance. And the accomplishments of the subjugated societies They created are legendary. Look at the Pyramids. Look at Rome or Teotihuacan.

Our forefathers, along with Celestial Pures, had been tasked with providing the impetus, guidance and motivation to further the advancement and development of Earthkind. While there have been significant advances in technology and nation building, most consider the recent moral, ethical and spiritual development of Earthkind to have recently taken a significant giant step backwards.

It is no secret that Earth Pures, like Ourselves, cannot understand mankind's almost inconceivable reluctance to acknowledge the truth which is so obviously staring them in the face; the fact that the Earth is *not* their planet of origin!

Non-pures have recently surmised that modern man suddenly appeared out of nowhere some ten thousand years ago. And although they may be off by as much as forty thousand years, they are correct in concluding that we absolutely did not evolve from Earth's cavemen or, incomprehensibly, from apes.

But the fact that today's scientists steadfastly refuse to admit that primitive man could not have built the magnificent monolithic ancient cities of stone or the glorious pyramids found all around the earth without Celestial help, is baffling.

The people living near so many of the ancient edifices are still, thousands of years later, incapable of recreating the works of their ancestors, even with today's so-called modern technology.

They persist in believing in their "gods and angels" while rejecting the existence of "Little Green

Men" and aliens. Well, We are not little or green like our Grey brothers, but We are most certainly here, despite the **Global Conspiracy** to cover up the truth.

After all, an **Angel**, by definition, is an **Alien**

Civilizations on every Earth continent, while completely unaware of each other, have consistently told the same story; that they were visited by "**Sky People**" who educated them, **mated** with them, producing "**Star Children**", and assisted in their spiritual and societal growth.

But how could the Sky People have successfully mated with Earth humans if They were not of the same species? Do Non-pures really believe that an advanced species would have sired children with apes? Doesn't anyone ever take the time to even consider the obvious?

The other common assertion of each and every one of Earth's colonies is that the Sky People, or **Star Beings**, as some referred to them,

assured them that they would **return** someday.

And, my friends, that day has drawn nigh.

This is the very first Summit for some of you, and so I will begin by introducing myself in the grand tradition of past Summits.

I, Australia, come to you today as the Leader and Chairman of this esteemed Council. I am the son of a Celestial Pure who is a direct descendant of the magnificent **Wandjina** the Grey,

as some of Us refer to him, who liberated the "Firsts" on the great continent of Australia.

My mother, an Aboriginal Pure, was taken up by my father's spacecraft, and received the blessing of motherhood from my Overseer father, who had admired her from afar for many years. It was He who oversaw the implementation of my enhancements and to whom I owe my esteemed position.

I am also here representing the countries of New Zealand, Tasmania, Papua New Guinea, the beautiful Whitsunday and Hook Islands, and by default, the Federated States of Micronesia, and Pohnpei, where the mysterious ruins of the ancient city of **Nan Madol,** which means the "space in between", were constructed on ninety-two artificial islets built on top of coral reefs around 1180 AD.

The channeled island's initial name was Soun Nan-leng, which surreptitiously means "the Reef of Heaven", but is also referred to as the "Venice of the Pacific".

Legend has it that the structures and altar were built by the twin Sub-pure sorcerers **Olisihpa and Olosohpa** to worship their god of agriculture, the Celestial Pure **Nahnisohn Sahpw,** Who helped them transport the megalithic stones from distant quarries and levitate them into place with the aid of His "flying dragon". It has been suggested that the scope of this task rivals that of the construction of the Egyptian pyramids.

Australia, an Original Drop Site, is the home of 10,000-year-old ancient architecture in Central New South Wales, the sacred **Bora sites** and of the wondrous **Kakadu cave paintings**, which crudely depict some of

Our Celestial Ancestors, and the fairy-like **Mimi spirits**.

The indigenous Aboriginal people are now and have always been a spiritual people. Our **Dreamtime** Spirituality is the stuff of legends, and can be traced back to the ancestral **Totemic Spirit Beings** of the Dreaming.

Our Dreamtime stories are still used to explain how the land and creatures were originally created.

Australia: Who would like to go next…Washington?

Washington: Pick somebody else. My throat is still sore.

Australia: Very well…Egypt?

Egypt: Gladly!

I, Egypt, unlike Australia, actually have something to brag about. I am the proud son of two
Egyptian Pures who are the direct descendants of the Celestial Pures
Osiris and Isis

and the great **Akhenaten** the Pure, Himself, husband to the beautiful **Nefertiti**

and father to the unforgettable **Tutankhamun**

I am also here on the behalf of Iraq, and the true Anunnaki connection of the **Sumerians** of Mesopotamia.

Marduk, a Babylonian **creation god**, and the son of **Enki** (Ea), gained prominence there by defeating **Tiamat**, the so-called "dragon" of the primordial sea who was once the leader of the Anunnaki gods, according to **The Enuma Elish.**

I stand proudly on behalf of Lebanon and its Original Drop Site **Baalbek,**

which was named to honor **Baal**, still another Celestial Pure; and later renamed **Heliopolis**, the City of the Sun, by the Greeks in honor of the Celestial Pure **Zeus.**

I am also here to represent Jordan and its magnificent city of **Petra**, the Rose City,

which was carved out of solid rock with the assistance of their local Celestial Pure Overseer, and is one of the seven wonders of the world.

I am also here to represent Syria and Iran with its famous **Pleiades Monument** and **star map**.

Let me not fail to acknowledge Saudi Arabia and the Holy City of **Mecca**, where Muhammad himself conversed with the Celestial Pure **Gabriel** some five-plus years after reportedly re-setting the **Black Stone** in the cornerstone of the **Kaaba.**

The Black Stone, believed by many to be a meteorite possessing supernatural powers, was said to be a gift from a Celestial Pure who instructed an Earth Pure (not actually Adam but possibly a direct descendant) to place it at an altar which He would occasionally visit.

Legend has it that after reportedly being lost during **Noah's flood**, the Black Stone was later recovered by **Ibrahim**, who received instructions from the Celestial Pure **Jibrail**, for it to be embedded in a new temple to be built by his son **Ismael** and dedicated to the Celestial Pure **Hubal**.

After several tumultuous incidents, the Kaaba is once again the place where the remnants of the Black Stone are paid homage during the **Hajj**.

Egypt is home to the unequaled **Pyramids at Giza.**

The Great Pyramid, claimed to have been built by **Khufu (Cheops)** or **Thoth** the Atlantean, aka **Hermes** (as reported in the **Emerald Tablets**), is where some of the first Earthborn Pures were temporarily buried; and where we can gape in awe of the magnificence of the precisely carved **obelisks,** the inexplicable symmetry of hundreds of Pharaohic statues, and the unmatched beauty and grandeur of the world-renowned
Great Sphinx of Giza.

And let Us not forget **Saqqara**, home of the **stepped pyramid of Djoser**, which stands along with the oldest complete stone building complex known to Earth Humans.
Its design has been attributed to the great, possible Earth Pure,

Imhotep,

who was reported to possibly be the son of **Ptah** and **Sekhmet**, two Celestial Pures. He was noted for being a renowned architect, statesman and Egypt's first physician.

All of these exceptional architectural achievements were accomplished with the technological expertise of Our ancestral Pures, and are still not duplicatable with today's inferior earthborn technologies.

I stand before you today, humbled by my heritage and swollen with pride.

Rome: I think I'm gonna be sick.

Australia: Well, before you do, why not go next.

Rome: I think I will, so that I can show this young upstart how to introduce himself, sans the braggadocio.

Britain: Hear, hear!

Rome: I don't need you to cosign, my dear.

Britain: Well, I never!

Rome: But of course you have. Even with me!

Britain: ... ...

Rome: As I was saying.

I, ahem, Rome, have the ear of the Pontiff himself. He never speaks without first asking for my opinion or perspective on matters concerning the laity.

I currently reside in the Vatican City, which, I must remind you, is its own country, and I care not who knows it. I am a third degree black belt and, like Russia, I have been trained extensively in the martial arts of the mind. And, unlike Russia, I know when and where to pick my battles.

Russia: Do I really have to sit here and listen to this pompous blowhard? Let Egypt speak again!

India, Britain, Ethiopia, Peru, Washington and Japan: *NO!!*

Rome: You wound me, sir.

Russia: I would like to! Just get on with it… and keep my name out of it!

Rome: Very well then. As I was saying. Ummm, what was I saying? Oh yes, Rome, an Original Drop Site, is the home of the Vatican, which may very well be the most esteemed place on the planet; even more so than Mecca. Lord knows we have a lot more money.

Anyway, Rome is home to the world's greatest religion, Christianity! We control the hearts and minds of millions upon millions of pathetic, gullible Mutes in every corner of the globe. We speak and they still listen! Our influence is all-pervasive! Our reach is all-encompassing, and our greed is insatiable!

And to think that it was all dreamed up by a Celestial Pure and His Taint of a Son!

All: Civility!!

Ethiopia: There is no way I am going to continue to sit through this. If he continues to denigrate Christianity, I will personally kill him! I'll wrap his third degree black belt around his throat and strangle him with it!

Rome: I'm sorry, Ethiopia, I mistook you for a Pure, not a Christian. You certainly can't be both!

All: Civility!

Ethiopia: You should thank God that Australia is restraining me; otherwise… You know what, Rome? I'll see you after the Summit…*pish…katta!*

Rome: Do you actually believe I'm afraid of you?

Ethiopia: You talk very large for a Taint! The rumors are obviously true!

Scattered: *I heard the same thing! Me too! It can't be possible!*

Rome: It isn't. And I promise you that by this time tomorrow, he'll regret he even suggested it. If he still has the capacity to regret anything at all.

Ethiopia: I'm sure that everyone here just heard you threaten my life. I will bring an entire continent down on your head if you even try to lay a vile thought on me!

Australia: Are you two little boys finished with your pissing contest? Do I need to intervene? Suffice it to say that the two of you won't be leaving here at the same time.

Rome: Was it something I said?

At any rate, I am also here to represent France and the great **Merovingian Dynasty,** which was founded by my ancestor **Childeric** the Pure, and his son **Clovis,** who was believed to be a Taint. Rumor has it that Childeric was acting against the better judgment of the Celestial Pures above, Who spent decades unsuccessfully trying to bring Him and Clovis to their respective knees. That's why He's my personal hero.

Corsica, France, is known for the megalithic site of **Filitosa** and its **Menhir** statuary.

Some state that Filitosa, as well as the **Tumulus of Bougon,** were known to be constructed by Mutes at the behest of local Earth Pures, and *without* the aid of their Celestial Brethren.

However, legend has it that many of the huge remaining menhir stones strewn throughout Europe were erected by a race of giants from 3,000 to 6,000 years ago, with limited help from the above Celestials.

I also proudly represent Greece and the Celestial Pures Who were hailed as the illustrious Gods of **Mount Olympus** by the Greeks and the Romans alike.

Who can forget their Tainted offspring **Hercules, Samson, Achilles, Theseus, Perseus** and so many others. The Pures were screwing everything in sight back then!

If only they'd turn Us loose now! It doesn't seem quite fair, does it?

The **Minoans**

were an advanced colony of Earth Pures and High-level Taints founded on the Isle of Crete.

Their King **Minos**

was the son of the Celestial Pure **Zeus** and the Earth Pure **Europa**.

— 23 —

The **Minotaur**, aka Asterion (slain by Theseus), was reportedly the result of a non-sanctioned gene splicing experiment, similar to those performed in Egypt,

conducted by the Celestial Pure **Neptune,** aka **Poseidon,**

who ruled over a submerged Pure Colony.

He reportedly used DNA from a white bull and Minos' wife, **Pasiphaë**, also an Earth Pure, who, along with her ancient witch sister **Circe**, were the daughters of the Celestial Pure **Helios** (aka **Sol**), who drove the "Chariot of the Sun"

across the sky, and the **Oceanid** nymph, **Perse**.

Helios' illuminated spacecraft was later destroyed in a fiery crash involving his reckless Earth Pure son, **Phaethon**, who was killed when Zeus shot the careening craft out of the sky, before it could set the entire Earth on fire.

Most of the Minoan Earth Pures were taken off planet during The Great Departure, when Their ornate palaces, at **Knossos , Phaistos, Malia,** and **Kato Zakros**, were intentionally destroyed along with many of the remnants of Their advanced culture, by disgruntled Celestial Pures, when ordered to leave.

Why everyone regards that entire era as pure myth is beyond me. But then, Mutes will believe just about anything...*except* the truth. Most don't even believe *We* exist, but they will when We bring the hammer down! Well...some will, anyway. I'm convinced that most are too dense to ever see the truth, no matter how obvious it is. They prefer to adhere to their comfortable little acceptable lies, no matter how preposterous, outlandish or improbable they may be. Gullible doesn't even begin to describe them.

Nero, the Christian-hating Taint, had the right idea. Why, even I have half a mind to.........

Australia: Half a mind is exactly what you'll have if you don't cease this endless tirade of disgusting animus. *Finish up, NOW!*

Rome: Yes sir, boss! (And don't ever do that to me again.)

As I was saying, and in conclusion; I am here to represent Italy, Spain and its ancient city of **Tiermes,** which was carved out of solid rock.

Germany, and its well-documented **UFO battle over Nuremberg 1561,**

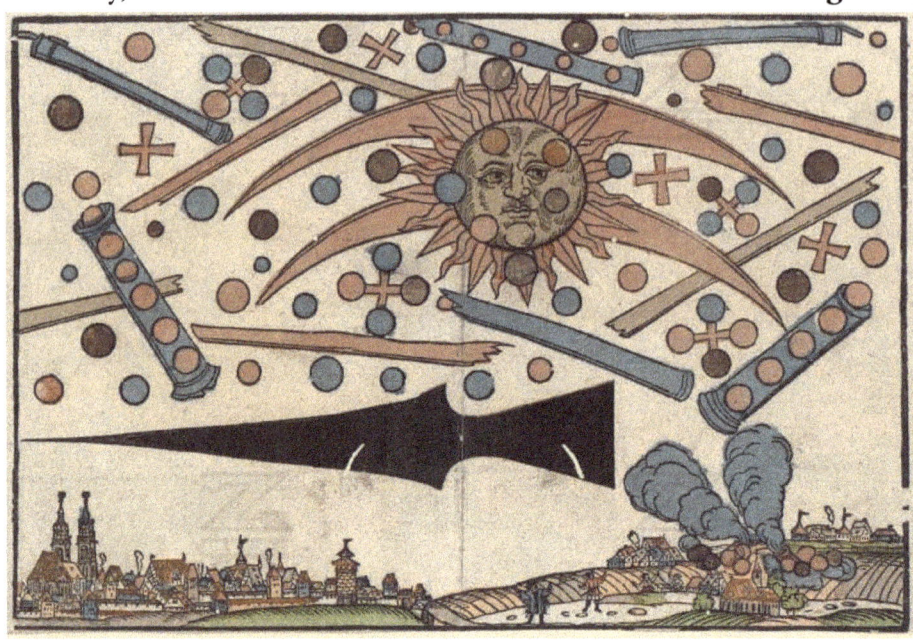

Portugal and Malta, with its 5,000-year-old megalithic temple complex of **Ħaġar Qim.**

The 57-ton stone found in the temple façade is the largest piece of limestone used in all of Maltese's many megalithic structures.

All fine, fine countries.

Lest I forget, I must acknowledge those like the famed Oracle at Delphi, who became an **intermediary between the, uh…Earth Human rulers and the Celestial Pure Apollo.**

As some of you may already know, the city of **Delphi** was once regarded as the center of the earth.

I find it interesting that Earth Humans today believe that Earth Humans three thousand years ago were foolish enough to build thousands of elaborate temples to worship "nonexistent" deities. And yet today they still build churches, mosques and temples to honor Jesus, Muhammad and Buddha, whom they have also never seen, and who never speak back to them during their prayers.

How does one square that in one's mind? It can't be easy. And please don't tell me it's because the new religions make any more sense than the old ones.

Lastly, the **Agora of Athens**, the **Acropolis**, the **Parthenon**, the **Coliseum**, and numerous other wonderful examples of stone construction were commissioned and oftentimes designed by Earth Pures.

Thank you for your feigned patience.

Australia: And thank you for your unsolicited spitefulness.

Rome: Ooooh! Sarcasm… I love it!

Australia: Who would like to go next? Japan?

Japan: Sure, why not. Maybe I can help get the vile residue of Rome's rhetoric out of everyone's psyche.

I, Japan, am the son of two wisened Japanese Pures. My father is a direct descendant of the first Japanese emperor, **Jimmu** the Pure, who was a direct

descendant of the first Earth Pures officially relocated to Japan as a Secondary Drop Site from an Original Drop Site in China, where they still resent our superior accomplishments to this day.

China: And, here we go!

Washington: *This should be good!*

Australia: Out loud and in English, please.

Washington: I'm just sayin'!

Japan: Mr. Chairman, I believe I have the floor.

Australia: Please continue.

Japan: As I was saying before I was so *rudely* interrupted…

China: You think that was rude? I'll show you rude…*ban…gaah!*

Japan: Your mother is a ban…gaah! Whatever that means.

China: That's it! Here and now, you son of a Mute!

Japan: Sticks and stones, Porky!

Ethiopia: Oh my God! You were right, Washington. This *is* good!

Egypt: Yeah, this is starting to feel just like back home!

Peru: Mr. Chairman, aren't you going to do something?

Australia: You mean, besides laugh?

Russia: Let them fight! Please!

Israel: Yeah, I'm in the mood for a little bloodshed!

Rome: I agree with Ms. Peru, Mr. Chairman… Choke them out!

Britain: Hear, hear! Civility!

India: My head is going to explode! Mr. Chairman, I must insist!

Japan: *Gotcha!* We got 'em good, China. We really had them going!

China:	We sure did! Why do they keep insisting that we must hate each other?
Japan:	I don't know. Maybe it's the eyes!
China:	You think? Well, mine *are* prettier than yours.
Japan:	Let me see, darling.
	Actually, China and I are good friends. We met while attending the same university in the United States many years ago. We are currently in the middle of some potentially very profitable business ventures.
China:	Yes, we are going to take over the entire planet! And you will all let us, because you are powerless to stop us!
Britain:	We'll just see about that!
Egypt:	Can I get in on this?
Rome:	Et tu, Brute?
Egypt:	Don't hate, participate!
Japan:	You were right earlier, Rome...but it isn't only the "Mutes" who will fall for *anything*.
China:	We got them again, my brother! This is too easy.
Japan:	It sure is! You guys gotta know that we wouldn't *really* try to take over the whole world...and actually tell you about it... Would we?
China:	Yeah, we'd come like thieves in the night, the way most of your countries used to take advantage of ours. Payback is a mother!
Britain:	Are you still upset about Hong Kong? We gave it back.
China:	We *took* it back. But thanks for nothing.
India:	Britain, you might not want to start this discussion right now. Not while some of us are pretending to have forgotten what your form of oppressive imperialism can do to a country.
Britain:	But *I* didn't personally have anything to do with any of that!
Australia:	That's what they all say.

Washington: Britain…just let it go.

Russia: Let it be noted that I stayed completely out of this discussion.

Japan: I'm sorry. I think I fell asleep for a minute. Where was I?

Oh yes, Japan wants the bomb!

No, that's not where I was…

In all seriousness, I, Japan, am also here to represent South Korea (*don't say anything, China*), the up-and-coming Malaysia, with its "**Microterrestrials**," (*I can't believe I even mentioned that*), the Philippines, where there have recently been numerous "UFO" sightings, and Indonesia, the home of the inexplicable **Candi Sukah**, with its obviously Mayan-influenced **Cetho Temple.**

Indonesia is also home to the astonishing **Borobudur Temple**, on the island

of Java, which consists of 2,672 relief panels, 504 Buddha statues, and is the largest Buddha monument in the world.

Even seeing is not believing!

Although constructed by Non-pures, the original design and blueprints were given to **Gunadharma**, an Earth Pure, by an unnamed Celestial Pure Overseer who loved to marvel at this true work of art, from above.

And I represent…the Senkaku islands.

China: You just can't help yourself, can you? Those are the Diaoyu Islands, and as you well know…

Japan: Mr. Chairman, I believe I still have the floor.

Australia: Mr. Japan still has the floor. Please continue.

Japan: Thank you.

As I was saying, our Imperial Dynasties are beyond legendary, and were largely established by Earth Pures who remained in constant contact with Their regional Celestial Pures. However, even They couldn't keep it in Their pants and many an Emperor fathered children with Non-pure concubines, which forever "muddied the waters," as one might say.

Like so many other countries, Japan is also the home of megalithic structures.

The **Ishibutai Kofun**

is topped by two granite stones, weighing 60 and 77 tons respectively, which, along with twenty-eight others, were quarried 1.9 miles away and moved to the sight of the tomb approximately 1,400 years ago with the aid of Pure technology.

Other carved structures include **Ishi-no-Hōden**

and **Masuda-no-Iwafun** (Rock ship).

Japan has a rich history of "UFO" sightings, which include the heavily

documented **Utsuro Bune**

encounters from 200-plus years ago, which detail a redheaded non-Asian Pure female of approximately twenty years of age, clutching tightly to a possibly wooden box, emerging from a flying saucer found floating in the Pacific Ocean. I kid you not. Look it up.

Higher circles have postulated that she had either escaped from an underwater Pure complex in an effort to consort with terrestrial humans, or that her ship had simply suffered technological problems and became disabled. Regardless, she soon disappeared along with the ship.

This pales in comparison to the 10,000-year-old Japanese lost underwater Pure City of **Yonaguni,** just off the coast of Okinawa. It's commonly called the **Japanese Atlantis**.

Many Japanese children are raised with tales of its underwater castles and the lost civilization that once inhabited these ruins. Most Japanese Pures believe the city was abandoned and sunk back in the days of the Great Leaving.

Top that, China!

China: I don't mind if I do.

Unlike my verbose Japanese amigo, I will try to keep this short and sweet

I, China, can trace my roots back to the great **Xia Dynasty**.

Japan: Yeah, and even to **Peking man**!

China: I am going to ignore that ungracious outburst since We all know that Peking man was not a Human and, unlike Us, was actually an indigenous life-form on this planet; not unlike **Neanderthals** and **Cro-Magnon man**, who were genocidally exterminated by Our forefathers with the help of Celestial Pures, as they posed a direct threat to Human safety and development. Not to mention the fact that some Mutes disgustingly kept trying to breed with them.

As previously mentioned, **Modern Humans,** or Earth Humans as we often refer to ourselves, **are not** the descendants of Earth's **prehistoric cavemen.**

**(See chart below)

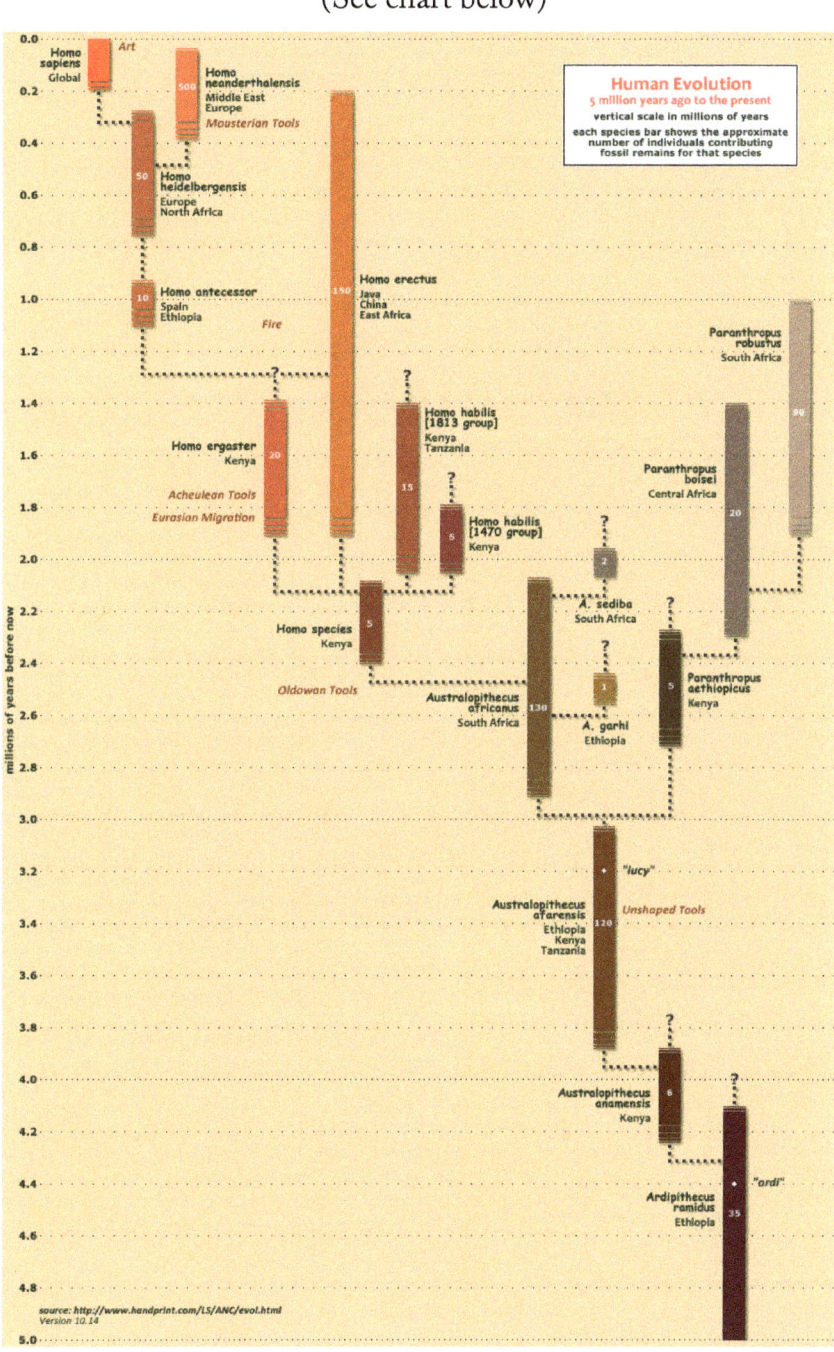

Nor were we "manufactured" by some god, or by a group of "spacemen." I'm sorry, I am a geneticist, and this topic always pisses me off! The **mitochondrial DNA** does not lie. Look it up. There is no "**Missing Link**," at least not here on Earth!

Now, hopefully without further interruption, I shall continue.

I can also trace my roots back to the **Yellow Emperor, Huangdi**,

who was also an Earth Pure on my mother's side. He is credited with the invention of Chinese medicine, the compass, the calendar and many ancient religious practices. He is still worshiped in some circles today.

As was customary, His remains were eventually returned to Our ancestral planet by the regional Celestial Pure Overseer, or "**Watcher**" as many call them now. Local legend, however, claims that he rode a "dragon" up to Heaven.

In addition, I am here representing Tibet, whose dedicated

Celestial Pure protector, **Chenrezig,**

also known as **Avalokiteshvara,** is their Buddhist embodiment of compassion. The eternal Lord of Love, Chenrezig vowed to eliminate the suffering of all beings.

I am also here to represent Thailand and Nepal, where the questionable
Lolladoff Plate

can be found. The plate's design clearly depicts a spiral galaxy, a Grey and a disk-shaped spacecraft, even though the plate is reportedly 12,000 years old.

Unlike Egypt, and a host of other countries, upon the Great Leaving, Celestial Pures ordered our people to cover their **Chinese Pyramids** with mud, dirt and plant life to discourage tomb robbers and mausoleum defilers. Many are still said to contain the world-renowned **Terra Cotta Warriors,** along with pottery figurines of silk-adorned female servants and domesticated animals. Some of these ancient burial mounds are still believed to contain the physical remains of revered Chinese Earth Pures.

Unlike many other subservient civilizations, the Chinese Earth Pures, Taints and Mutes collectively revolted against the Celestial Pures who posed as Sky Gods, enslaved us, and forced us to help them build Their pyramids and landing sites like the infamous

Xianyang Pyramid,

aka the "**White Pyramid.**" We still aren't sure what the elaborate collection of reddish brown metal pipes They deployed were supposed to be sucking from the earth.

A bloody **Ancient Chinese/Alien War** ensued that lasted for centuries.

Legend has it that twelve-foot-tall **Redheaded Giants (Nephilim?)**

in leather armor from the north helped us win the war and to free ourselves from Celestial tyranny. I wouldn't mention this if it were not well documented and verified.

Lest I forget, the reportedly 12,000-year-old mystery-shrouded **Dropa Stones** are supposedly remnants of a crashed spacecraft bearing a diminutive race of people with large heads and eyes who called themselves the **Dropa**. Just sounds like it was a group of stranded Celestial Pures to me.

Our **Great Wall of China**

was commissioned by the **First Emperor Qin Shi Huang**, an Earth Pure who formed the first Conglomerate Dynasty and unified China.

Our Pure Chinese heritage is rich, and like other civilizations, despite the efforts by "Some" to erase the truth, that heritage remains carved in stone and encapsulated in our ancient pyramids.

Australia: Excellent. Who's next.

Washington: I'll go next.

              By the way, Mr. China, you and your friend Mr. Japan over there, don't sound very "Asian" to me.

China: We so sorry for dat, Mr. Washington. We try harder to "prease" you next time.

Japan: Good one!

Washington: Hey, I didn't mean it as an insult or anything.

All: That's what they all say!

Washington: Never mind. I guess this dreaded "political correctness" is all-pervasive nowadays.

Anyway, I, Washington, am currently a presidential consultant and the proud descendant of the Celestial Pure **Gici Niwaskw.** My heritage can also be traced back to the renowned

Native American **Chief Powhatan,**

(**Wahunsenacawh**), one of the last known "Indian" Pures, and the father of **Pocahontas**.

Japan:	How!
Washington:	What do you mean how? Through DNA testing.
Japan:	No, no. I was just saying hello in "Indian"!
	(Laughter by All)
Washington:	Touché! Point well taken. You guys are a tough crowd.

I am a proud member of the NRA, a master in several martial arts, and a retired Navy SEAL. I have been to Area 51, touched the spacecraft, and actually held a couple of the artifacts. I'd say more, but I'm being told, in my head, not to, by our illustrious Chairman. If anyone has a problem with me…Bring It! Uh, except you, Mr. Chairman. And I really do want to know where I can acquire some of those kickass enhancements you've got.

I am also here representing the great country of Canada, which includes **Oak Island**'s infamous **Money Pit.**

Despite the rumors and speculation that have persisted for over 200 years, I have it on good authority that the Money Pit was originally the construction of a Celestial Pure who was hoarding Earth artifacts and treasures.

The "pit" itself was originally dug using matter displacement equipment aboard his spacecraft, and the lowering of the treasure was witnessed by some local Mute fishermen who later tried to dig it up using an elaborate system of picks, logs, and flagstone. Countless others over the centuries have tried, failed, and oftentimes died seeking His treasure.

Now, I've been told that the Celestial Pure who planted the treasure there has long since recovered the bulk of it, abandoned the booby-trapped dig, and returned to His home planet with His pilfered booty. All of this is purely conjecture though, even if it is intriguing as hell.

The "alleged" treasure in the Money Pit most likely consisted of artifacts like those supposedly found by **G.E. Kincaid** in a cave he discovered in the Grand Canyon in 1909. This, too, is yet to be verified.

The contents of the cave were reported to have been mostly Oriental and Egyptian artifacts, some of which appeared to be tablets inscribed with hieroglyphics. Other copper objects, weapons and "mummies" were also retrieved and allegedly shipped to the **Smithsonian Institution** in Washington, D.C., where they were never seen or heard from again.

What I've been told most likely happened, was that a Celestial Pure took a temporary workforce of Egyptians to the Grand Canyon to dig a series of virtually inaccessible cave passageways and rooms wherein He could conceal His growing collection of confiscated artifacts from around the world.

Later, some of these caves were expanded and inhabited by a group of ancient Hopi Indians who subsequently were spared annihilation from a forewarned regional catastrophe.

Many Hopi still believe in **The Blue Kachina prophesy**, which tells of the return of the **Star Beings** in Their "flying shields," and of Their "Purifier," **The Red Kachina**, who will bring about the end of the **Fourth World**.

During The Great Departure, the aforementioned Celestial removed his most prized artifacts from the caves and abandoned the rest, which is what G.E. Kincaid discovered centuries later.

Those who believe that the entire story is just a legend or hoax, and that the American government would never cover up the truth, should remind themselves of how the *Roswell Daily Record* newspaper had quoted several eyewitness sources concerning the capture of a crashed **Flying Saucer** in **Roswell, New Mexico**, only to retract the story the next day, claiming that it was only a "weather balloon." Who's being naïve now?

I am also here proudly representing the great country of Mexico and its
Mayan cities of **Chichen Itza,**

where the pyramid of **El Castillo** still regally stands;
Calakmul, the **Kingdom of the Snake**, where we find the awe-inspiring

Great Pyramid of Calakmul;

and the once Earth Pure-run colony and multi-ethnic **Teotihuacan**, the **"City of the Gods,"** which was "discovered," not built, by the Aztecs, with its

illustrious **Pyramids of the Sun and Moon,**

and the human sacrificial **Temple of the Feathered Serpent**, beneath which

liquid mercury has been inexplicably found,
and the **Avenue of the Dead,** along with beautifully vibrant murals**.**

All of this was constructed by Pure craftsmen (possibly Igigi) before it eventually became one
of the Original Mute Drop Sites

How can I not mention the awesome
Aztec City of Tenochtitlan, which is now a part of Mexico City itself,

and **Uxmal** with its beautiful **Pyramid of the Magician.**

There are just too many to make note of here, but I would be remiss if I failed to mention the
"ancient astronaut" **Pakal** the Pure, and His newly restored

Maya city of **Palenque**

in southern Mexico, with its beautiful **Temple of Inscriptions.**

There is an actual sculpture there of **Pakal**

inside what appears to be a spacecraft, found on the lid of a sarcophagus.

And the **Toltec** city of **Tula de Allende** with its magnificent pyramid and **Atlantean Figures**.

Then there is the **Guatemalan Temple at Tikal,**

Caracol, in Belize

and **Xunantunich** in **Belize.**

Somebody please stop me!

There are so many more, and they were all inspired by, constructed by, designed by, or commissioned by Celestial and Earth Pures who exploited the physical labor of the local Mutes. Yes, they were in fact good for something!

Ladies and gentlemen, my eyes tear and my heart swells with pride when I think of the contribution Our kind has made to this dreary planet. We have indeed made it a worthy addition to Human history throughout the known universe!

Scattered: Bravo! Well said! Hear, hear! Right on!

Washington: Right on? Never mind.

It is believed that the great **Montezuma I**, the Aztec emperor who consolidated the Aztec empire, was indeed an Earth Pure, but his son and heir, **Montezuma II**, was at best a low-level Taint who had no telepathic skills at all, and thusly was proffered no aid whatsoever from the regional Celestials when his cities were invaded by

Cortes and his barbaric **Conquistadores**

who brought an inglorious end to the Aztec empire.

So much for preserving the bloodline.

Panama, which I represent, is rumored to have been one of the original sources for gold and copper mining by some of the early Celestials Who enslaved the local populace and imported Earth Pures from other continents to oversee Their enterprise.

Rumor has it that Earth Pures were the first to commission the building of the Panama Canal, also employing slave labor. However, I haven't been able to verify this as of yet.

The Great and lofty United States of America is home to **Monks Mound**, known as the North American pyramid. Its base rivals that of the Great Pyramid at Giza and is larger than that of the Pyramid of the Sun; but because it was constructed solely by Mutes, of soil and clay, it is slumping and collapsing in places. Apparently this is the best that can be expected from Mutes, without the aid of Pure planning and technology.

Monks Mound is also one of the sites in North America where the skeletons of giants with **double rows of teeth** have been unearthed.

Conversely, the 10,000 to 15,000-year-old **Pyramid Lake Petroglyphs**

discovered in Nevada, were obviously made using Celestial Pure carving tools. Modern-day scientists and archeologists are stymied, to say the least, because all of their nonsensical theories about supposed

Human migration patterns

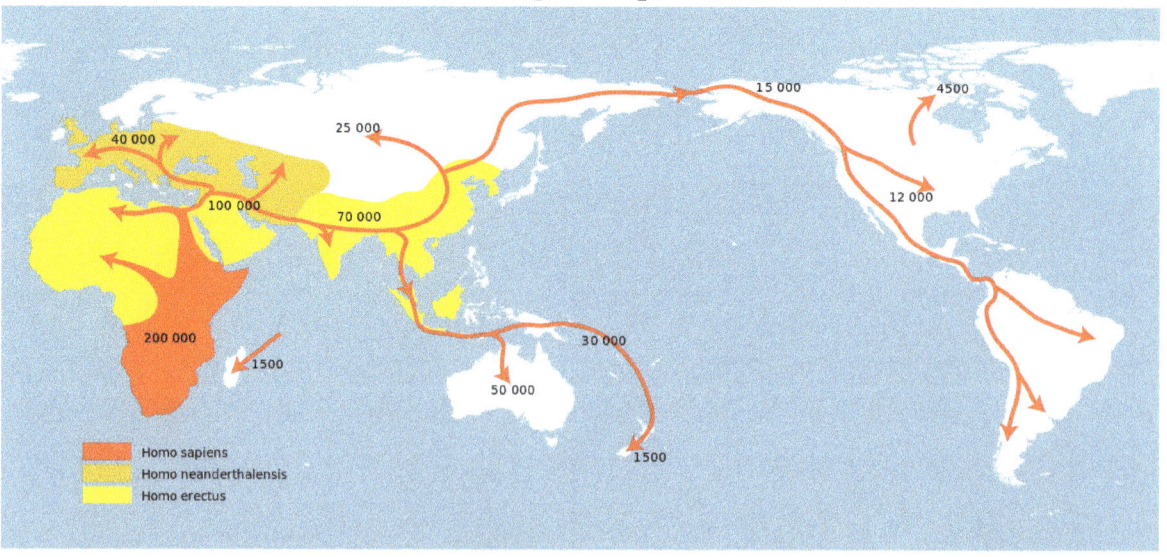

and early Human developmental capabilities are finally being called into question.

Ancestral Human Beings *never* migrated that way on Earth. And then, on top of it all, somehow managed to change their skin color, hair texture and color, eye color and race? C'mon! Stop it!

"The more we think we know, the more we find we don't.", to quote some songwriter.

Heck, I'll even give a shout-out to **Ed Leedskalnin** for building the only known modern monolithic site he called **Rock Gate Park**, all by himself,

using some of the Celestial electromagnetic antigravitational techniques he was secretly taught and, as instructed, refused to pass on to others. Today they call the site the **Coral Castle** down in Florida.

The **Anasazi** of **Mesa Verde**,

along with other **Ancient Pueblo Peoples**, suddenly turned from being hunter-gatherers to cliff dwellers, at the direction of their local Celestial Pure Overseer. They were assisted in developing new stone housing construction and agricultural techniques which included water channeling and dam building.

The eventual departure of the rain-producing Celestials resulted in a prolonged drought, which led to the abandonment of the sites and the migration of the Pueblo cliff dwellers to less hostile environments.

I am also here to represent the ominous **Bermuda Triangle**, where a known deep-sea Celestial Pure Base is still located. And, in addition,

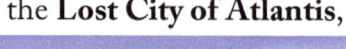

the **Lost City of Atlantis,**

which many claim was evacuated and then sunk during the Great Departure, while others insist that it merely "took off" back into space, not unlike the mythical "continents" of **Lemuria** and **Mu,** which many believe were actually submerged motherships.

Britain: You can't claim those, you pompous idiot!

Washington: Well, somebody has to, and I just did, Witchypoo.

Britain: This is my last warning. Better still, I shall take the floor.

Rome: Like you did in Vegas?

Britain: Shut up, ingrate!

Rome: Oh, please don't get me wrong. I was grateful!

Britain: Let it be noted that I have only been with four men in my entire life, and that being with you was the last time I will ever engage in pity sex.

Rome: Ouch!

Britain:	Mr. Chairman, please call the room to order.
Egypt:	I'll have a cheeseburger please!
Japan:	Pizza for me!
China:	Got any popcorn?
Britain:	I give up. You're all idiots!
India:	Really?
Britain:	Well, except for you and Ms. Peru and possibly Mr. Ethiopia and the Chairman, of course. My apologies.

I, Britain, am the offspring of an English Pure father who is the direct descendant of **King Arthur** the Pure, and an Irish Pure mother, who was the direct descendant of the renowned

Merlin the Pure.

The *real* Merlin the "warlock," whose actual name I shall not disclose to the likes of you, and not the largely contrived wizard Merlin of myth.

Like my mother before me and her mother and grandmother, I, too, am an **Irish Traditional Witch**.

Japan:	Are you for real, lady?

Britain:	Are you….. E.T.?

I'd be glad to prove it to you, but I doubt that Mr. Chairman over there would permit me.

Let me make something perfectly clear. To Mutes, **Telepathy** is **Magic. Levitation** is magic. **Psychokinesis, Astral Projection, Clairvoyance, Precognition, Psychometry, Remote Viewing** and **Psychic Reading** are all "magic." But most if not all of you are somewhat proficient in many if not all of these arcane practices. Am I not right?

Non-pures would be also if not for the mutated genes they possess that robbed them of these abilities long ago. Fortunately, the **FOXP2** language gene was spared, preserving their power of speech.

For more than seventy-five years, Non-pures have known that they use less than 50% of their brains. It is obvious to everyone that animals with brains one-thousandth the size of the human brain can function well enough to communicate, mate, build, raise their children, feed themselves and organize communities.

Although some of the Non-pure brain has been reassigned more mundane tasks to perform, all of the aforementioned diminished brain functions were meant to be prevalent aspects of the evolved Human brain.

It is a shame that we have not been able to reinvigorate these brain functions in Non-pures. Remnants still exist, but the deficiencies seem to be permanent and, sadly, nonreversibly inheritable.

Take any one of these higher brain functions, throw in a little herbology, chemistry, pharmacology and apothecological science, and you have a "Witch."

Today's magic is tomorrow's science. If you want to see *real* magic, just look at your "Smart Phone."

Most Non-pures are somewhat aware of all of these schools of mental prowess because they themselves have either personally experienced them or have been witness to them to some lesser degree. Mr. Australia has apparently had his abilities artificially heightened. By definition, that would make me *much* more normal than he is.

Australia:	Gee, thanks a lot! That bus just rolled right on over me and kept on going.

Britain:	My point is that all of you would be judged as Witches or Magicians by Non-pures. I'm not all that different than most of you. (Just wiser and more adept.)

Russia:	Did you say something?

Britain: I was just saying that the Isle of Great Britain was a Secondary Drop Site initiated as an experiment by a Celestial Pure, whom some believe to have been **Woden (Odin)** himself

He had hoped to set up a royal hierarchy of **Lumainian** Pures from the colony on **Hy-Brasil**

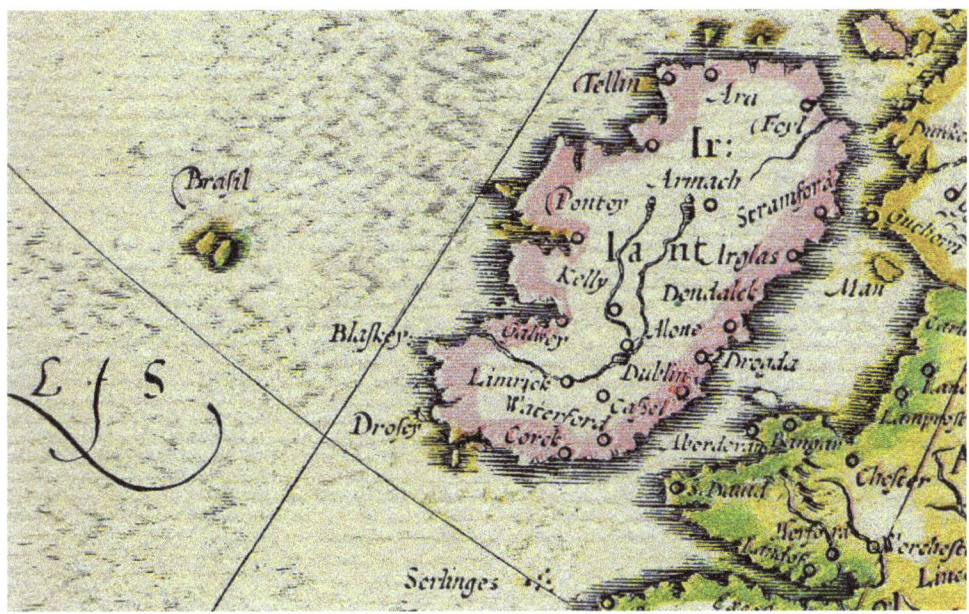

to rule over the filthy barbarians that had found the island and were wandering around aimlessly killing each other. Hy-Brasil was also abandoned and supposedly sunk off the coast of Ireland during the Great Departure.

That hierarchy still exists today, but the Royal Blood has been badly diluted due to unrestrained lust and lies. There are a few high-level Sub-pures or Taints, as some of you call them, left walking around; but most aren't even aware of who they are or what they are potentially capable of. Sad, isn't it?

Unlike most of you, Britain can lay claim to current proof that Celestial Pures are still up there observing everything we do, and actively engaging us.

Proof , you ask?

Crop Circles,

a few of which were actually made by Celestials, and the rest by copycat Mutes.

Perhaps our most famous Celestial Pure designed and commissioned Megalithic artifact is the world-renowned 5,000-year-old

Stonehenge.

Originally part of a Pure Colony, this ancient monument is aligned with the winter and summer solstice. The 40-ton blocks were transported twenty miles to the site using a Celestial spacecraft.

I would also like to acknowledge the recently discovered and older **Superhenge,** and the 4,000-year-old Neolithic Mute construction, **Woodhenge.**

I am not only representing England, but also Ireland, where the ancient
Tuatha De Danann Pures once ruled.

They were reportedly a royal tribe of Earth Pures who were rumored to be immortal. I actually met one of their descendants years ago. He was an arrogant fop who cursed me out for not giving him the time of day.

I also represent Belgium, Wales, Norway and **Switzerland**, where a minor skirmish between Celestial Pure spaceships was witnessed, reported and recorded on **woodcuts in 1566**.

Then there's Sweden, where even to this date, several Swedish Pures still insist that they are the direct descendants of **Freyr**, another Celestial Pure who feigned godhood.

It's a shame that their ship-shaped megalithic monument, the **Ale's Stones**, were not better preserved. Each stone weighs in at about 1.8 tons.

Denmark, an Original Drop Site, was once ruled by an Earth Pure called **Gorm the Old**, apparently because he couldn't stay awake; and later by his Taint son **Harald Bluetooth**, whose beloved mother **Thyra**, a warrior, was claimed to be the daughter of both the King of England and the Jarl of Jutland. Apparently her Taint mother got around quite a bit.

This stuff is just too good to be made up.

The famed **Jelling Stones** were raised to honor Gorm and Thyra.

The Netherlands have a hodgepodge of lineages due to the fact that their land was in flux for centuries. They're known for Holland, being Dutch, and having windmills and wooden shoes; but many try to wrongfully associate them with the Vikings, the Norse Gods and other Northern Germanic traditions that don't necessarily fit.

Anyway, I'm here to represent them, and Greenland, where the Eskimo, Saqqaq, Dorset, Thule, Viking, Icelanders and Norwegian cultures all went to die. Denmark, sadly, tries to rule it today.

The **Norse Gods** were an extended family of Celestial Pures who, during a power struggle, wreaked havoc upon the northern Germanic tribes until They were physically forced to cease and desist. There, I said it.

Their mothership, the **Asgard**,

was equipped with extensive observational equipment, and **Odin**, the regional Overseer, sought to rule through intimidation and false promises of immortality in **Valhalla** for those who fought in His name.

Apparently **Loki** and **Freyja** wanted to share His power and, along with numerous other Celestials, were known to come down to Earth to "stir the pot" on a regular basis.

Thor, another Celestial Pure, was tasked with keeping the peace on **Midgard**, as They called it, and with fending off **Ragnarok**, which was a planned genocide by Odin to bring new order to the unruly barbaric Mutes below.

As I previously alluded to, other Celestial Pure Overseers, with explicit orders from Their home planets, intervened and forced the Asgard to eventually return home, where many of the so-called "Gods" were demoted and had Their Celestial Visas revoked.

The historically semi-factual temporary rule of the "Norse Gods" was almost immediately relegated to the status of Myth, just two generations after Their departure. Why so many other similarly contrived religions persist, is beyond me.

Great Britain is the birthplace of a myriad of fairy tales and mythical creatures like Leprechauns, Ogres, fire-breathing Dragons and Fairies.

This has readily contributed to making it very difficult for Non-pures to make a clear distinction between what is real, like Us, and what is purely a concoction of someone's vivid imagination. And because We have been forbidden to disclose Our very existence, We must regrettably continue to bite Our collective tongues whenever the subject of **Extraterrestrials** comes up.

I, for one, don't understand why We don't just call a press conference and get it over with!

Australia: Because Non-pures have a nasty habit of not believing Us when We do. Not to mention the threat of being taken off planet for extensive counseling.

                And you do remember the **Salem Witch Trials**, don't you? They've made it very clear that they don't trust Us or Our agenda.

Ethiopia: Should they?

Australia: Point well taken. I don't know. Would you like to go next?

Ethiopia.   Of course. I'd be honored.

                I, Ethiopia, am here to represent far too many proud African countries to enumerate. Exactly what they are proud of, I am not at all sure.

                That was a joke, people!

Scattered: *Oh! I thought he was being serious. He was telling the truth, wasn't he? I thought he'd made a valid point.*

Ethiopia: Enough!

                I, Ethiopia, am the proud descendent of

the Earth Pure **King Lalibela** himself!

I need say nothing else, but I will!

It was King Lalibela, a Saint, mind you, who was escorted up to a mothership by the Celestial Pure **Gabriel** himself, to meet with the Regional Overseer, who commissioned him to build eleven churches by hewing them out of solid rock.

Legend has it that although the daytime labor was performed by Non-pures, as those workers slept, Celestial Pures, probably the Igigi, came down at night and also worked on the churches.

It is scientifically conceded today that the churches could not possibly have been constructed without the help and the tools of the Celestial Pures.

My heritage can also be traced back to **King Menelik** I the Pure, the son of the great Earth Pure **King Solomon**, and **Makeda** the Pure, also known as the beautiful **Queen of Sheba**.

It was King Menelik who brought the **Arc of the Covenant** from **Jerusalem**

to Lalibela in Ethiopia. It was later moved to **Axum**, where it is rumored to still reside in the **Church of Our Lady Mary of Zion** to this day.

Before I continue I would like to say something.

My beloved half-brother, a Sub-pure, or Taint as some of you would call him, had himself implanted with "Grey Market" Celestial Pure Tech, or C.P. Tech as we refer to it, in order to better telepathically communicate with other Pure family members and friends.

After six months he began complaining that We were all "psychically shouting" at him and that he could no longer shut Us out. He became violent and suicidal, and it was the Christian Church that took him in, counseled him, and ultimately saved his life!

He has since had the C.P. Tech removed and is currently studying to be a priest at one of the Lalibela churches.

Now, I may not be a Christian myself, but I have many friends and associates who are, and I try to respect that, as difficult as it may be. So tread lightly on the subject, please.

As I am sure some of You already know, it was the **Olmec**, a Negroid race of Earth Pure Igigi descendants from Africa, Who were transported by Celestial Pures to **San Lorenzo and La Venta, Mexico**, around 1500 BCE, to help jump-start their civilizations. This preceded the founding of Rome itself. Later, both the Maya and the Aztec cultures directly profited from Olmec tutelage.

Most Olmecs were eventually taken off planet during the Great Departure, although many claim that some were actually relocated to Polynesia. They left behind Them pyramids (which were not built in west Africa), Their famous ball courts, and numerous gigantic **Olmec Heads** (which are also not found in Africa) as proof of Their inhabitancy.

These stone heads were displayed nearly a hundred miles from their source, and scientists today still cannot ascertain how the huge boulders were moved onsite without the use of oxen or the wheel. But We know, don't We? The 6 to 50 ton heads were levitated to their sites using Celestial technology.

Few know that the ball game **ulama** (Maya - Pok a Tok, Aztec - Tlachtli),

which the Olmecs played, was originally brought to Earth from Their **ancestral** planet.

Although today it is propelled by the hip, initially, the heavy rubber ball had to be kept aloft and mentally thrown through the highly elevated vertical stone hoops via **telekinesis**, and without the use of any body parts.

It was originally designed to help the Pure youth to further develop their telekinetic skills, but after being taken up by Sub-pures, it devolved into a lengthy, grueling, brutal game which saw the eventual winner willingly sacrificed to their absentee "gods" (who had suddenly abandoned them during the Great Departure), in the hope that the human sacrifices would encourage Them to return. Needless to say, They did not; and years later, the conquering Spanish either banned the deadly game completely, or oversaw the extensive rule changes.

The **Vadoma tribe** of Zimbabwe, or "ostrich people" as some call them, are sometimes born with five fingers on each hand but only two toes on each foot, which is a dominant trait they claim to have inherited from a species of birdlike beings from the Sirius star system who came to Earth and mated with their ancient ancestors. Well, if true, it certainly wasn't Us.

Mali, an Original Drop Site, which I also represent, is home to the **Dogon** tribe.

The Dogon people have always held to the belief that they were visited by an extraterrestrial race of amphibious beings called the **Nommo** who came here from a planet that revolves around **Sirius B** or possibly Sirius C, which is a companion star to **Sirius A**, but cannot be seen by the naked eye.

Scientists are astonished that the Dogon people could have this information, along with knowledge about Saturn's rings and Jupiter's four moons, without the use of telescopes.

Well, I'm sure that We've all been made aware of the fact that there **are** other races and species out there that have also mastered space flight. After all, the Celestial Pures have always insisted that They have remained in close contact with the Earth to protect Earthkind from hostile alien invaders.

So, being a physicist as well as an astronomer myself, although I admit that I remain skeptical, I cannot rule out the possibility that there is some truth hidden amongst the Dogon's volumes of nonsense and confusion.

It should come as no surprise that once again modern-day scientists have taken some very surprising and borderline absurd leaps of faith in order to explain what they believe is inexplicable.

The first of these I shall point out is **Mitochondrial Eve**. I am trying my best not to gag at just the thought of it; but even the concept of supposedly tracing all Modern Human lineage back to a single primitive Earth female, is so preposterous as to not warrant any further consideration. What about Eve's mother and her four sisters?

I guess when they don't have any cogent answers, they just treat pure theoretical speculation as if it were the truth, no matter how improbable it may ultimately prove to be.

Secondly, the inane concepts of **String Theory** and **M-Theory...** please tell them to come back when their respective grants run out and they decide that they are ready to be serious.

Next is the abject ridiculousness of some of their carbon-14 dating and other badly flawed methods of determining how long ago something took place, or how old something might be; in particular, stone.

I understand that this method may be the best they have at the moment, but to use those tests to assert that the **Ancient South African Gold Mines** may be 160,000 years old, is borderline irresponsible. My brain may burst from my skull!

The speculative methods used to come to these conclusions are both frivolous and intellectually bereft of certitude. So, why then publish these obvious inaccuracies? Did they ever consider that the stones in the ancient stone calendar (some call **Adam's Calendar**) may have been shifted by a previous crustal displacement?

Listen, it has been made clear to me that the first visitations to Earth were made somewhere around 50,000-plus years ago. The first Drop Sites, which were established thousands of years later, were said to include no more than three hundred to five hundred Non-pures apiece. Some as few as twenty-five.

The first gold mines, however, were reportedly excavated 50,000 years ago under the supervision of The Celestial Pure **Enki**, by the **Igigi/Igigu,**

a lower caste of Anunnaki; assisted, reportedly, by Giants.

Centuries later, after growing weary of the seemingly endless hard labor, the Igigi eventually rebelled and refused to continue the gold extraction.

Once their numbers had significantly grown at the nearby Original South African Drop Site, some of the Non-pure (**Adamu**) population were re-enslaved by Enki's brother **Enlil**, at the behest of their Father

Anu, the "King of the gods,"

and forced to resume the task of exhuming the gold reportedly needed to augment the failing atmosphere of Their "home planet" **Nibiru**, with its nonsensical 3,600-year orbit. The truth is, Nibiru is most likely a Mothership, not a planet. Common sense should tell you that any planet would freeze completely solid and extinguish all life if it indeed ventured that far from its sun.

Other Non-pures hunted, gathered, built shelters, fetched water and took time out to bear children...... but not 160,000 years ago as postulated! Just move the displaced astrological stones a little to the right!

Sorry about that, but there really is no excuse for this level of ineptitude posing as pseudo-science.

Egypt: Calm down. It'll be okay. Now, why don't you tell us how you really feel?

(Scattered laughter)

Ethiopia: I thought I just did.

(Scattered laughter again)

Ethiopia: China, it may interest you to know that **two hundred Giant Alien Skeletons** were reportedly found in a cemetery in **Kigali, Rwanda**. I remain skeptical, however, so I've been making plans to personally look into this further.

Australia: That was a very thought-provoking presentation, Mr. Ethiopia. Thank you.

Next?

Israel: I'll go next.

I, Israel, am the direct descendant of...wait for it...not Jesus Christ!
Moses, the Earth Pure

who was born to **Jochebed**, an enslaved Hebrew Earth Pure whose own mother was an undisclosed Celestial Pure. Moses' biological father was a Celestial Pure Overseer who sought to free the Israelites from His predecessor's complicit servitude.

Let me explain.

It is recorded that the regional Celestial Pure Overseer Yahweh (YHWH) had "encouraged" the new reigning Egyptian King to enslave the immigrant Hebrews, whose population was growing in numbers that threatened to ultimately surpass those of the Egyptians themselves, so that the construction of His cities and pyramids might be expedited.

The King, or Pharaoh, as some referred to him, had also been provided with the technologically advanced tools of the Celestials that were necessary to hew, carve and transport the needed construction materials.

Over the centuries, a number of additional atrocities took place, such as the sanctioned killing of the firstborn sons of the Hebrews, to further suppress their population growth. To no avail, the Hebrews protested and petitioned for their freedom.

Moses, the Royal adopted son of the King's daughter, fled Egypt and was later recruited by His Celestial Father, **Adonai** (who had replaced **Yahweh**) to reluctantly return to Egypt and free his brethren from enslavement.

Armed with the technology of His Celestial Father, whose tacit "involvement," in the form of 10 orchestrated plagues, eventually persuaded the Egyptian King to comply, Moses gathered his fellow Hebrews and migrated north to eventually reclaim Israel.

Along the way, the Israelites proved themselves to be ungrateful and disloyal to their newly self-appointed "God", who summarily impeded their return until His own ego was appeased by their eventual praise, respect and subservience. Once again they found themselves dictated to by an unrelenting and unforgiving Master from above.

Moses, the loyal and obedient son, was eventually taken aboard his Father's spacecraft, where He spent the remainder of His days in relative comfort.

Centuries later, **Imman**, or **Jesus**, as most know him, was instrumental in altering the Israelites' relationship with his own Celestial Pure Father, **Avinu**, who, also posing as Yahweh, established a **New Covenant** between them.

It is still disputed to this day as to whether or not Jesus was an Earth Pure, or a mere Taint who had received enhancements from his "Heavenly Father." It is well documented that his mother, Mary (supposedly an Earth Pure, but was most likely a Mid-level Taint) was artificially inseminated with the sperm of Avinu, by Celestial Pures, locally referred to as angels, acting on His behalf; which adequately explains Jesus' "virgin birth."

And, by the way, the **Three Wise Men**, **Magi**, or Kings, as they were referred to, were obviously Earth Pures led by Avinu to Bethlehem to honor his son Imman's birth.

It was always Avinu's plan to "resurrect" his Son, Imman, as pseudo-proof that by worshiping Him, Non-pures would somehow be granted immortality.

Together they fashioned the far less oppressive **Christianity**, which vastly grew his Father's base of worshipers by permitting non-Hebrews to finally participate. This brilliant move alone has resulted in one of the greatest surviving and thriving religions on Earth.

To my surprise, the **Shroud of Turin**,

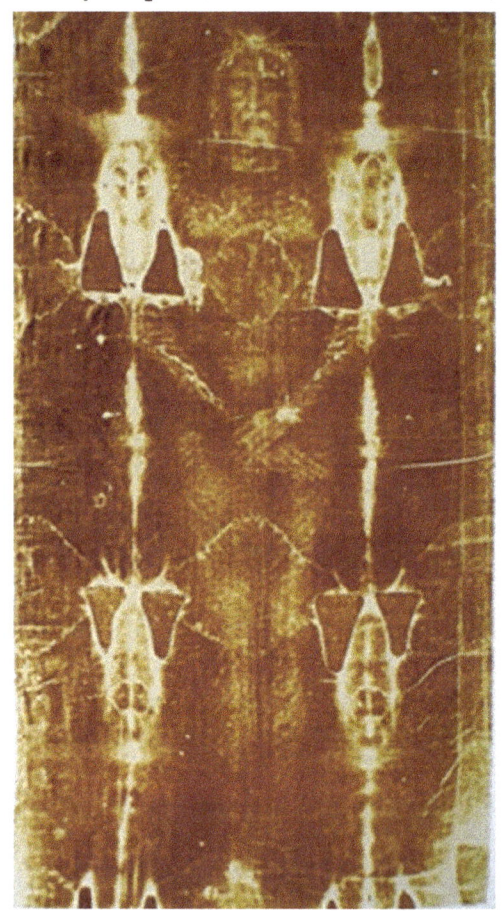

although it still has not been authenticated, is believed by many Pures to be the real deal.

Rumor has it that Avinu used Celestial Technology to "**resurrect**" his heavily sedated Son in the tomb, and that the device He waved over him actually caused the faint image of Imman to appear on the fabric itself, while altering the fabric on a sub-atomic level, causing current carbon dating attempts to give false readings.

Sometimes techno-logical explanations can prove to be the best.

Like Moses, Jesus was also taken off planet (ascended) and eventually transported to his Father's home planet, where he and his Father eventually passed away.

By the way, **Adam and Eve** were Sub-pures who were the pet project of a Celestial Overseer, believed to be **Enlil**, who sought to establish a new Colony in His privately sequestered **"Garden of Eden."**

At the time, there were already *many* considerably larger Non-pure colonies all over the globe, such as the one in the unruly **Land of Nod**.

Enki, aka **Lucifer**, an Anunnaki Pure, who was **Enlil**'s half-brother, felt sorry for Adam and Eve's repressed intellectual capacities, and sought to enlighten them by administering a counteragent to the stupor-inducing drug the Overseer had been using to anesthetize them.

Enraged, Enlil incarcerated the compassionate Enki, and, after casting them out of Eden for their disobedience and disloyalty, punished the couple and later, their sons, **Cain and Able**, with hard labor.

Later, Enlil made a deal with Enki/Lucifer to free Him, if He would continue to test the faithfulness of His Non-pure followers by taunting and tempting them. This ill-conceived practice ended with the Great Leaving.

I guess I'm finished, since I don't represent any other countries.

Australia: Thank you for the sermon, Mr. Israel. Ms. India, would you like to go next?

India: Most assuredly.

I, India, am the proud descendant of the Earth Pure **Siddhartha Gautama,**

the **Supreme Buddha,** who was born in Nepal to the Earth Pure

Queen Maha Maya, who was artificially inseminated by **Vishnu.**

Brahma

Shiva

It is said that the name Shiva means "The Pure One"; not to be confused with The **Three Pure Ones** of **Taoism**.

Vishnu, an Overseer, was, like so many other Hindu deities, obviously a very influential Celestial Pure. He was often erroneously portrayed as having blue skin and four arms by some artist who took creative liberty after the reports of a sighting.

As you know, true Pures would never defile themselves in that way. However, it is reported that Vishnu liked the depiction because it temporarily set him apart from other Celestial Pures, and so, initially encouraged it.

Although his story sounds very similar to that of Jesus the Christ, Gautama the Buddha was born over four hundred years earlier. In fact, it is touted that it was the success of Siddhartha's Celestial father Vishnu, in reforming **Hinduism into Buddhism**, that was the main catalyst for Avinu's efforts to morph **Judaism into Christianity**; a religion fashioned to honor both Him and His Earthborn son.

Unbelievably, The **Kailasa Temple**,

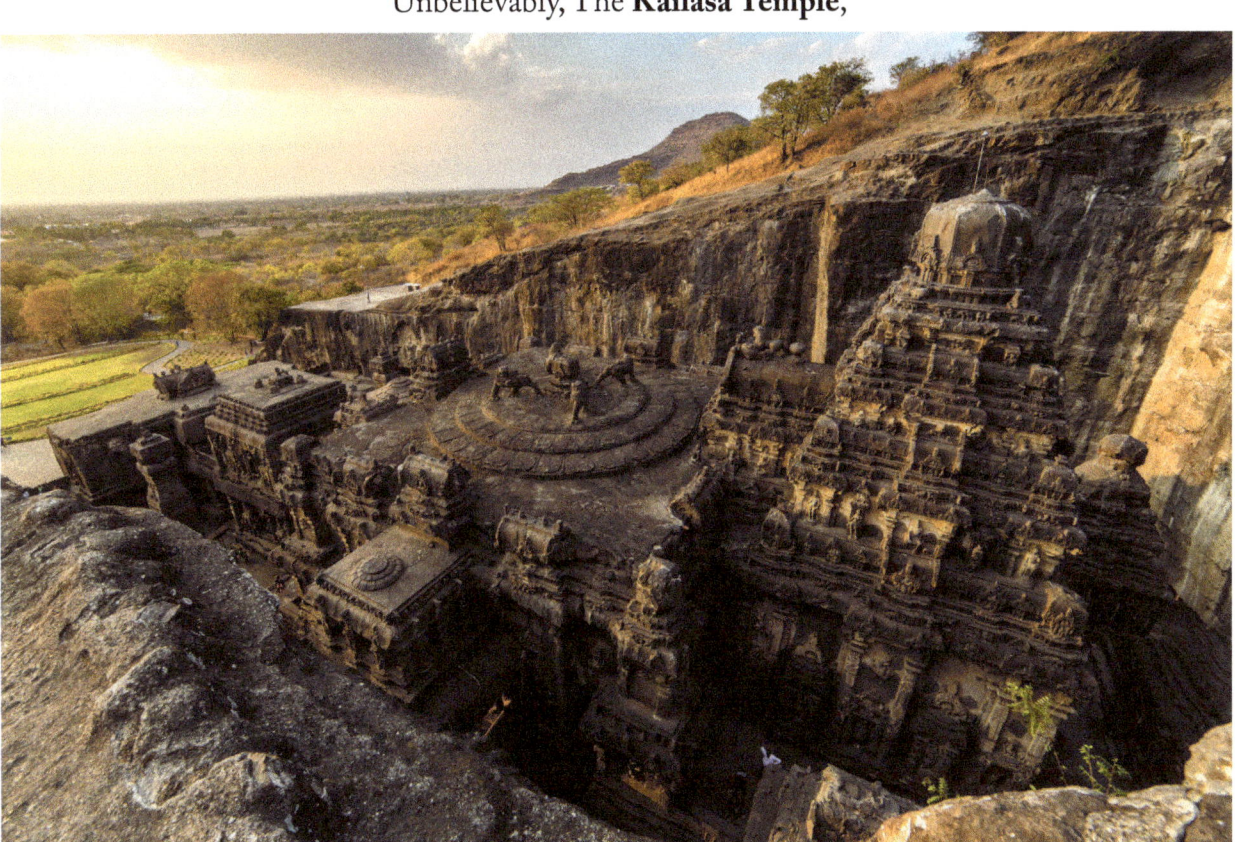

some call the **"Home of Lord Shiva"**, was carved out of a single stone.

In the Hindu epic poem **"Ramayana"**, the Celestial Pure **Rama** rescued **Sita**,

his Earth Pure wife, by building the now submerged bridge **Rama Setu** between India and Sri Lanka, approximately ten thousand (not a million as some believe) years ago, which can still clearly be seen from space.

I am also here to represent Cambodia and its magnificent temple
Angkor Wat,

which was built by **King Suryavarman II**, who was reportedly a Sub-pure who received his architectural blueprints from **Preah Pisnokar**, who was the offspring of a Non-Pure father, **Ta Seng**, and a Celestial Pure mother, **Tipsoda Chan**, who was a possible descendant of Vishnu himself.

In addition, I represent Pakistan, where a rogue Celestial, having made a mining deal with the Aryans who were fighting against the Mongols, agreed to use an ancient spaceship called a **Vimana** to drop what was then the

equivalent of an **Atomic Bomb at Mohenjo Daro** approximately 4,000 years ago, in what is now Pakistan.

This event is also reported in the famous **Mahabharata,**

an epic **Sanskrit** poem which also tells of the **Kurukshetra War** and the direct involvement of **Krishna,** a flute-playing Celestial Pure who sided with the Pandava Prince **Arjuna** and imparted upon him the **Bhagavad Gita,** which later inspired the great **Mahatma Gandhi** himself.

Recently it has been reported that a **5,000-year-old Vimana** spacecraft has been found in a cave in **Afghanistan**. It is said to be protected by a "strange energy barrier."

It is believed that the ship may have belonged to the Persian Prophet **Zoroaster** (aka Zarathustra), an Earth Pure who received a vision from the Celestial Pure **Ahura Mazda** and later founded **Zoroastrianism**.

The Romans called Zoroaster the inventor of magic.

I have yet to verify this story, although it has been widely reported.

My region is also responsible for the formulation of not only **Hinduism** and **Buddhism** but also **Jainism** and **Sikhism**.

Australia: Thank you very much, India. Russia, would you like to go next?

Russia: Only if I must. I admit that I have actually learned a few things today… Like how easy it is to bore the hell out of me!

I am joking, I am joking, people. Why is nobody laughing?

All: …………..

Russia: Okay, be like that and see what it gets you! I have no feelings to hurt.

I, Russia, am a Celestial Pure. Bow down to me!

Not even a chuckle? To Hell with you all!

I, Russia, am a direct descendant of the mighty **Rurik** the Pure, who was a famous **Varangian** chieftain. I'm sure that some of you have heard of him.

Scattered:	*Not me. Who did he say? Rubik's Cube? He's kidding again, right?*
Russia:	(*Imbeciles.*)

As some of you know, Russia is the home of the archeological site of **Arkaim**, the Russian Stonehenge in Siberia, which is believed to be 1,000 years older than Troy.

I'm sure you've all heard that in 1948 we also had our own **Kapustin Yar** UFO Crash, like that of the famous Roswell incident.

No? Well, how about the mysterious **Caldrons** they discovered in the **Valley of the Dead** that blew that freaking meteorite out of the sky before it could strike my beloved homeland?

Come on, comrades, these are all proof of Our Celestial brothers' ongoing obsession with Russia.

Would anyone like to discuss **Metatron's Cube**, the Celestial's **Flower of Life**, and how Russian scientists have discovered that if you take an icosahedron and flip it inside out into the dodecahedron and plot all of the applicable points on Earth's planetary grid along with the original 12 points of the icosahedron, you will have a worldwide grid that plots every single monolithic structure in the history of the world?

All:	(Loud laughter) He's kidding, right? That was the best joke he's told so far! Bravo, you really had me going for a second there! Kudos, my friend. You got me that time! He's such a kidder!
Russia:	Silence! I was being dead serious!
Japan:	Really? That's too bad.
Britain:	You're kidding now, right?
Ethiopia:	I confess, I can never tell when he is joking and when he is not.
Russia:	I give up. You all win. I know I am just a sad stuffed shirt with no friends and a badly inflated ego, but if you will all just…*kiss my big Russian ass*, I'm sure I'll feel better in no time!
All:	Laughter and applause.

Russia: I am also here representing the country of Turkey and their Neolithic sanctuary **Göbekli Tepe**,

which has been perched upon the top of a mountain range in all of its glorious splendor for 11,000 years. Well, okay, I'll admit that the site had been completely buried for centuries in an effort to preserve it.

From what I have been told, it used to be a place of meditation for a group of Earth Pure Igigi Who were praying to be taken off planet and returned to Their ancestral planet. This was, in fact, accomplished during the Great Leaving, at which time, with the aid of Celestial Pures, the site was buried like so many other Pure colonies so that it could not be used by the encroaching Mutes.

Derinkuyu, Turkey, is home to an extensive underground city, ordered built by the Celestial Pure **Ahura Mazda** to protect the local populace from a rival Celestial Who was threatening to exterminate them if they did not all renew their religious allegiance to Him. What an ego!

Nemrut Dagi, in Turkey, is home to the **Hierotheseion,**

which originally displayed Apollo, Tyche, Zeus, Antiochus I, and Heracles.

It was built by **King Antiochus I,** who counted himself amongst the gods, in conjunction with the Celestial Pure **Mithras;** and what began as an Earth Pure colony was later converted into a mausoleum.

I was asked not to discuss the **Bosnian pyramids** because they apparently don't exist. This includes the imaginary **Bosnian Pyramid of the Sun**, the **Pyramid of the Moon**, the **Pyramid of the Dragon**, the **Pyramid of Love** and the **Pyramid of the Earth.** Like I said, I won't talk about them, so don't ask, and don't look them up. They're just ordinary four-sided hills…with tunnels.

I am here to begrudgingly represent Germany, whose Nazis nearly won World War II by using stolen Celestial Technology.

Unbelievably, they actually built a flying saucer called the **Haunebu** that actually flew.

It was widely reported that Hitler was obsessed with the occult and all things "extraterrestrial."

In **Romania,** the **Coliboaia Cave Paintings** are estimated to be close to 30,000 years old, which would make them the oldest ever found in Central Europe.

What, exactly, that has to do with you and me, I don't know. Except that Neanderthals didn't paint.

The Hungarians want me to tell you that they believe that they are the direct descendants of the Anunnaki because their language bears the most similarity to the ancient Sumerian language. But I won't.

Zorats Karer, or the **Karahunj Observatory** as it is officially called today, is oftentimes referred to as the **Armenian Stonehenge**.

Some of its stones weigh up to 10 tons. It is estimated to be 7,500 years old, which would make it 4,500 years older than the English Stonehenge.

Even I must confess that the wall carvings seem to portray **Celestial Greys.**

Well, much to my regret and I am sure to your delight, I believe I am finished.

(Scattered laughter)

Australia:	Now that's the way to win over a hostile room. "In sooth, mostly goodly done."
	Peru, it's your turn.
Peru:	Do I *have* to go next?
Australia:	Well, since you're the last one, I believe you do.
Peru:	Well then, tell Mr. Egypt to stop "pinging" me, and to stop staring at me!
Japan:	Ooooh, busted!
Peru:	You're no better, Mr. Japan. You and your buddy China have been ogling my breasts since the moment I arrived.
China:	Well, if you don't want us to admire them, then maybe you should try covering them up!
Rome:	No, no, don't do that!
Britain:	Children, behave yourselves!
Rome:	Maybe you should take me in the other room and spank me...Please?
India:	Mr. Chairman, stop smiling and call the room to order!
Washington:	I'll have the foie gras.
Israel:	Unleavened bread and butter, please.
Russia:	Caviar for me!
Ethiopia:	Got any milk, Ms. Peru?
Peru:	*Yan pros skandra pru...usss!*
Scattered:	Oh my! I don't believe she just said that! Anybody got a bar of soap? What's my mother got to do with this? What did she say, what did she say?
Australia:	Order. *ORDER!*
	Thank You. Please continue, Ms. Peru, with **Our** apologies.

Peru: Please forgive my inappropriate outburst…. but I was brutally raped as a child.

All: Oh, I'm sorry to hear that.
           I didn't know.
           It must have been one of those lowlife Mutes.
           Now I really feel bad.
           Please forgive my earlier comment; it was totally inappropriate.

Peru: Are You kidding me? No man would *ever* get away with putting his hands on me!
           You guys really will fall for anything! Now, let's get back to business.

           I, Peru, am the direct descendant of the Celestial Pure **Viracocha**,

who, with the help of Igigi artisans, built one of the most complex and intricately beautiful
Earth Pure colonies in the world, at what is now called

Puma Punku, with its multi-alien-cultural **Wall of Humanity**, in **Tiwanaku**, Bolivia.

Viracocha personally transported the huge megalithic stone blocks, some weighing in excess of 100 tons, to the site using the anti-gravitational implements aboard his spacecraft, which he kept submerged inside a temple beneath the waters of **Lake Titicaca**.

Scientists today still can't believe the intricate work of the Pure artisans who meticulously carved the stones and precisely fitted the huge boulders together like a jigsaw puzzle. The nearby Incan tribes have always insisted that they did not construct the original 15,000-year-old complex, but rather discovered and temporarily inhabited it.

Unfortunately, Viracocha destroyed his work in a fit of rage, when He was ordered to abandon the site during the Great Departure.

It is said that he refused to return to his home planet following the Great Departure, and instead chose to wander the earth with his sons, continuing to teach and dole out wisdom.

was once believed to be the most ancient city of the Americas, and has been dated at somewhere around 2000 BC. But recently, **Bandurria, Peru**, has been dated to 3200 BC and is believed to have been an original Drop Site.

I remain in awe of the magnificent **Moai** on Chile's Easter Island.

Any fool can see that the Mute clans of the **Rapa Nui** could not have erected these wonderful statues along the coastline without the help of a rogue Celestial Pure and his advanced technology.

And the solid stone statues obviously didn't "walk" to their platforms, as the legends suggest. Clearly, the Celestial allowed them to use an anti-gravitational device to levitate, transport and place them there.

And any fool should also be able to see that it would have been quite impossible for these primitives to have found Easter Island two thousand miles off the coast of Chile, by themselves. And to assume that they found their way all the way back home in a canoe or a catamaran to bring their families there? *Viracocha!* Mutes can be so stupid! They were obviously dropped off there by a Celestial Pure!

When the Celestial Pure in charge was recalled, and the Rapa Nui found themselves subsequently abandoned and virtually cut off from the mainland, which was their primary source of food, they turned on each other, resorted to cannibalism, and proceeded to cast down some of the Moai statues in defiant frustration.

I am also here to represent Belize and Honduras, because they didn't care for Mr. Washington's smug attitude when they met with him. So, yes, Mr. Washington, just sit there and smile like the pompous ass that you are.

Honduras is the home of the ancient city of **Copan**

which was founded by **K'inich Yax K'uk' Mo',**

an Earth Pure who was reassigned from southern Mexico to develop and rule over the area. Believe it or not, he oftentimes wore glasses, due to his being quite nearsighted, some 1,500 years ago.

In 1996, **Varginha, Brazil,** was reported to be the crash site of a craft bearing three to seven extraterrestrial Greys, two or more of Whom were reportedly captured alive by the Brazilian military.

Although there were over 100 witnesses to the incident, I haven't heard anything about it since, which means that **NASA,** the global cover-up machine, and its so-called **Men In Black,** are still working overtime.

The inimitable **Nazca Lines,** in my beautiful country of Peru, have stymied the worldwide scientific community for years. Many just cannot accept the obvious. They'd rather believe that those mountaintops just leveled themselves.

They'd rather believe that whoever created those **geoglyphs**

on the mountainsides and in the desert, most of which cannot be seen from the ground, were just kicking rocks around for the hell of it.

They'd rather believe anything rather than believe that We exist. And I am personally getting really tired of the jokes and the insults I hear from the people I meet that don't realize who or what I am. I just wish they'd lift these stupid restrictions and let me speak out!

Australia: Don't do it. You just said yourself that the Greys that recently crash-landed have not been heard from since. I promise you that if you speak out, you'll either end up in an insane asylum or on an autopsy table.

Peru: I'd like to see them try that!

Forget what I just said. I'm just blowing off steam.

Anyway, the truth of the matter is that the Nazca people had an agreement with their local "God," probably Viracocha, that He would provide them with water to irrigate their crops if they would make these "etchings" for Him.

It's that simple.

While the geoglyphs were being created, He would take one of the workers He'd put in charge, up in His spacecraft and give him a detailed diagram of what He wanted and where He wanted the next figure to be.

When the Celestial left, during the Great Departure, the crops dried up and the Nazca people left the area. It's really not that hard to comprehend.

Several ships would regularly commune at the **Nazca Landing Strips**

that the Celestial Pures created Themselves, by leveling mountaintops, to brag about and compare the progress of their disparate patronages.

The nearby geoglyphs—unlike the multi-continental Celestially created, encoded crop circles—were merely commissioned as markers made for the amusement of the visiting Celestials.

The world's greatest archeologists today have become increasingly skeptical that the 9th century **Killke**, or the 13th century **Inca** alone, precisely carved and stacked the thousands of megalithic stones, weighing as much as 200 tons apiece, without mortar, modern tools, or machines, into the walls of

They are right to be skeptical, because the Incas openly admitted that their **Space Brothers** built it, and not them.

The awe-inspiring serenity of **Machu Picchu**, also known as the

Lost City of the Incas, however, is my personal favorite. Once an Earth Pure colony, it is pristinely situated atop a mountain ridge above the **Sacred Valley**. I personally give anonymous contributions to an organization that is currently having the site restored.

The 6,000-year-old **Ingá Stone** of Brazil

depicts carvings of figures, animals, fruits, the constellation Orion and the Milky Way. Many believe that it is a message left behind by our Celestial ancestors. Maybe They'll explain it to Us one day.

While I'm at it; although some of you no doubt have met an Earth or Celestial Pure with an **elongated skull,** I have not.

It is my understanding that this trait was not that unusual two or three thousand years ago.

In Peru, we apparently had a colony of them living in the **Paracas** region who surprisingly had European and Middle Eastern DNA. Go figure.

I have been told that during the Great Departure, most Pures with this trait were taken off planet or relocated to hidden Pure Colonies. This was done for two reasons. Firstly, because elongated skulls were not at all prevalent in Mute families, and secondly, because without the protection of the Celestials, they feared that these people would ultimately be singled out by ignorant, narrow-minded Mutes and possibly attacked and killed.

The Pures that remained on Earth, like our ancestors, could better blend in with the Mute population, who oftentimes resented the sudden departure of their Celestial "benefactors." In other words, many justifiably felt like they'd been ungraciously, unceremoniously and unjustifiably abandoned by their once dependable Gods.

It amazes me that so many Mute tribes all over the world sought to emulate this trait by binding the heads of their children to mimic an elongated skull, in hopes that some may think the child was "Celestially special."

In conclusion I would like to add that I also represent the wonderful countries of Argentina, Colombia, Ecuador, Paraguay and Uruguay, among others. All of these countries have reported an increase in UFO sightings of late.

Why is this? Is there something I'm missing?

Australia: Actually, yes. But before I explain, I would like to acknowledge the fact that due to a confluence of terms and idioms which are regionally but not globally prevalent, I have detected a modicum of confusion in some of your minds. Therefore, I will take a moment to clarify a few things so as to address any potential misunderstandings that may have arisen during our introductions.

I'll try to keep it simple.

As many of you know, "pinging" is commonly used as a means for one Earth Pure to identify another. By sending out a telepathic "ping", one hopes to receive a "pong" response, usually followed by a smile. In some circles a "ding" is sent and a "dong" is received, and in still others, it's a "tick" and a "tock." All are considered acceptable non-intrusive methods of Pure acknowledgment.

If done correctly, Non-pures can seldom hear them and Sub-pures that may hear them usually have not been trained as to how to respond to them. Subsequently, they tend to turn around looking confused and wondering if in fact they'd actually heard something, and if so, where the sound may have come from. Some of You take great delight in intentionally teasing them this way.

Now, on to more serious subjects. **The Greys** are supposed to be Us.

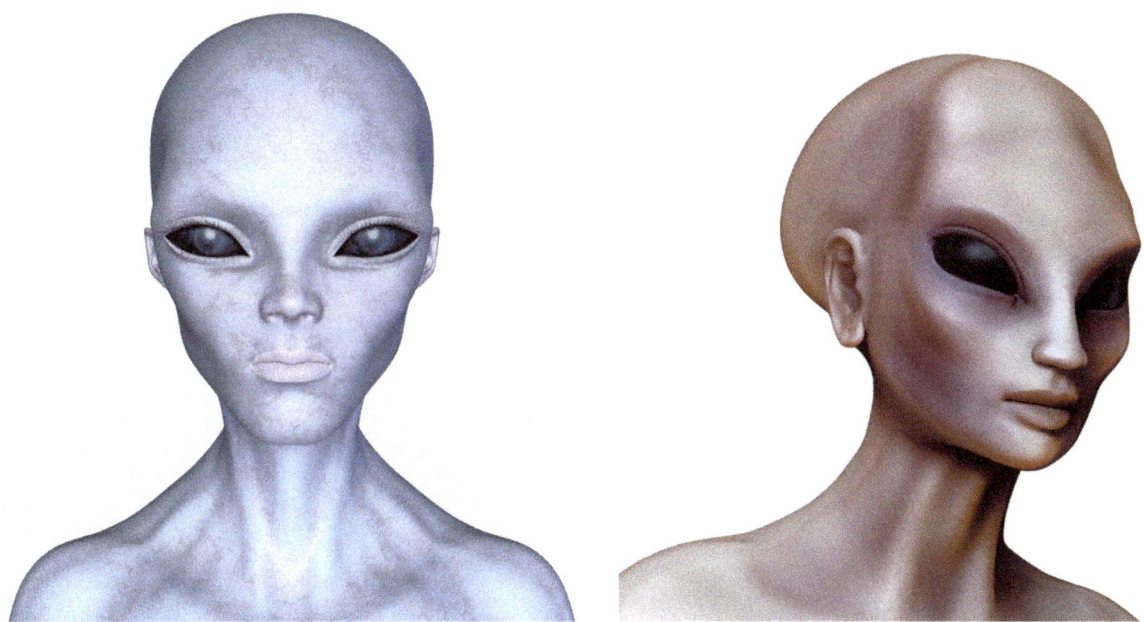

I have been told repeatedly that although They no longer look like Us, inside where it matters, beneath Their second skin, which covers Their almost nonexistent genitalia, They are mostly made of artificial organs, bone and skull fortifications which are meant to protect Their technologically preserved human brains.

So, should We still consider Them human? I say yes, because that is what They still consider Themselves to be. At least that is what I have been told, and I have observed no questionable activities on Their part to suggest otherwise.

Due to the physical sacrifices They have made, They are much better equipped to be "**Watchers**" than Their Celestial Pure predecessors. For one thing, Their physical makeup requires very little nutrition and has been proven to sustain Them for as long as 1,500 to 2,000 years of age. The lifespan of your typical Celestial Pure, like **Methuselah**, is around 500 to 1,000 years, and as you know, Earth Pures are expected to live no longer than 125 years. Although of late, We believe that number may be reasonably extended to 150 years, with the proper added supplements.

Their extended age expectation allows Greys to remain stationed here on Earth for centuries at a time before returning home for routine maintenance or "physiological retirement."

The "**Grey Market**" was established by a group of Greys who wanted to procure certain artifacts and/or Earth substances but, by edict, could not risk being seen or exposed. In exchange, They are willing to trade Celestial Pure Technology, or C.P. Tech, with a select number of Earth Pures.

Celestial Pures are Humans who were born on Their native planets, and not here on Earth. As a rule, They still live aboard Their spacecrafts, or on motherships which serve as Celestial and sometimes Earth Pure colonies today.

Earth Pures are just that, Pures, like Ourselves, who were born here on Earth.

A "**Taint**" is a derogatory term for a **Sub-pure**, meaning they have more than 10% mutated DNA and therefore somewhat diminished, although not totally absent, higher mental faculties. Some profess to be clairvoyant, some precognitive, and others are exceptional in one or two given areas of mental acuity.

High-Level Taints (**Star Children**) have corresponding IQs of 140 and above. **Low-Level Taints** bottom out at around an IQ of 110. However, there are also some Mutes with IQs as high as 120. Occasionally a notable Mute, oftentimes with some degree of autism, may exhibit extraordinary mental acuity in one specific field or another.

The **Illuminati**, as some of you intimately know, is a worldwide clandestine organization composed of Mid- to High-Level Taints who are being directly influenced, consciously and/or subconsciously, by Celestial and Earth Pures. They specialize in the infiltration of scientific and political organizations and the manipulation of world affairs. Although prohibited, it is widely believed that the organization also consists of a few scattered members who are "non-compliant" Earth Pures.

A "**Mute**" is a **Non-pure** who lacks most, if not all, of a specific set of advanced mental skills. The derogatory term Mute was derived from the presence of a specific mutated genetic structure all Non-pures possess. However, some take it to simply mean that they cannot "thought-speak" or use telepathy, and therefore they are technically "mentally mute." Some say the term M.U.T.E. actually stands for "Mentally Unable To Engage."

With a little effort We can thought-project into their minds so that they can "hear" Us when We want them to; and with little or no effort, We can hear what they are thinking without them being able to block Us out in either case. I like to say they lack "Mi-Fi" or "Me-Fi"; terms which are short for mind or mental fidelity.

When I use the term **Earthkind**, I am usually referring to all Humans born on the Earth; whether they are Pures, Sub-pures or Non-pures.

The Celestial and Earth Pures with elongated or bulbous heads, like some Greys, usually originated from a different home planet than Our own ancestors did, but We are otherwise very much alike. We now have relatives in the **Orion**, **Cygnus**, **Sirius**, **Pleiades** and **Zeta Reticuli** star systems.

None of Us, or Them, come directly from the planet of Our origin because it was destroyed thousands upon thousands of years ago during the "**Great War**" that led to Our Exodus and instigated the permanent mutations that are still prevalent and evident in Non-pures today. Let me clarify. During the **Exodus**, precipitated by the Great War, many of Our ancestors were exposed to trace levels of a since banned form of radiation, while others received life-threatening doses and/or obvious radiation burns.

Many died en route to one or more pre-designated planets that were already predetermined to be life-sustainable for Our Human species, just as the Earth was later determined to be.

After We arrived at the new planets, it was noted that some of Our species were giving birth to children with a radiation-initiated genetic mutation that ultimately robbed them of their capacity to use telepathy, levitate and to perform many of the other normal higher mental functions most of Us take for granted. Otherwise, they were, in all other respects, exactly like Us.

Due to their diminished capabilities, they were given most of the physical labor to perform, which included the building of Our new cities on Our new home planets, which shall remain nameless.

Centuries later, Non-pures were treated as little more than slaves, because Our communal sensibilities towards their plight had died along with those who had lived through the self-imposed holocaust of Our ancestral past.

Eventually, the "Mutes" revolted, and We placed them in the equivalent of reservation camps, where they needed work visas to even walk the very streets of the cities that they and their forefathers had paved.

Suddenly one day they decided that enough was enough, and they broke out of their encampments and began the bloodiest coordinated multi-planet revolution Our new worlds would ever experience. In Our circles it is still commonly referred to as the "**Mute Wars**."

The Peace Agreement/Covenant we entered into contained a promise to find the Mutes their own planet where they might live in peace and harmony, without the disdain and forced servitude We had subjected them to for millennia.

Earth, a mining planet for many centuries, was already sparsely populated by pockets of working class Igigi, who lived in established Pure Colonies along with a few other edible, domesticated species imported from the various home planets of their origin. But, as promised, Earth was re-designated as the new home of the Mutes. Their paradise. Their Eden.

For thousands of years, the already racially diverse First Drops were kept segregated from each other for safety—and to avoid a single unforeseen extinction event—on the different continents and/or hemispheres that most closely mimicked the climate of their respective home planets. This resulted in the further development of racially identifiable genotypes and phenotypes.

The "Firsts" quickly discovered that there were several other indigenous species of primitive humanoids already living on the Earth. Some were what are now called **Neanderthals** and **Cro-Magnon Man**, who many Pures believe were what was left of even earlier Drops, whose own evolution was permanently stunted by intentional abandonment and effusive inbreeding.

Others were reportedly giants with flaming red hair, and still others are what we now call Bigfoot and Yetis, who fled to the mountains and forests to escape our protracted efforts to completely eradicate their kind as a viable threat. Apparently they have long communal memories, because they wisely still go out of their way to avoid us to this day.

At first there was a sincere effort to live together with these other species, but as our numbers grew and some local resources began to dwindle, small skirmishes followed by all-out wars ensued. They were no match for us.

However, this time We didn't abandon the Non-pures. Instead, the Overseers from the different home planets hovered above Their perspective Drop sites to make sure that Their charges were properly fed and housed and received medical care until they became self-sufficient. Those who resented Our intrusive presence and persistent involvement in their affairs eventually moved away from the Drop Sites and out into the forests, caves and mountains.

Thousands of years later it was determined that the Earth Human population had grown substantial enough to sustain itself without Our additional and increasingly unwanted or unappreciated help. But many of the Overseers saw this as a prime opportunity to re-enslave their local Non-pures through threats of violence, coercion, outright lies and the intentional decimation of their food and water resources.

After the first few thousand years, there were no Non-pures left who had not been born on Earth, and subsequently, they did not know their own true history or even, for that matter, what a Celestial Pure was. As far as they collectively knew, Humans had evolved on Earth since their inception.

When the Celestials realized this, many of them exploited the Non-pures by posing as "Gods" and by concocting various "**creation myths**" to make Their charges believe that they owed their very existence to Them. After all, what the Gods had given, the Gods could certainly take away at will.

Not all of the Overseers behaved in such an irresponsible manner. Many reminded Themselves of the **Covenant** that originally brought the Mutes to Earth, and refused to participate in the madness that ensued.

Many Overseers entered into a kind of undeclared contest, where They competed to see Who could build the largest most elaborate cities, monuments and temples named after and/or dedicated to Themselves. This competition continued unabated for thousands of years.

Many of Them bestowed King and Queenships upon Their offspring and tasked them to rule over the unruly Mutes with iron fists. Mating with a Mute was considered an acceptable perk, but only the offspring of two Pures were initially permitted to ascend to the throne.

Dynasties were born all over the planet. Religions abounded. Every new Overseer sought to find a way to leave His mark upon the Earth. And all at the expense of the often starving, lowly, downtrodden Mutes.

Centuries later the decree came down from the home planets to cease and desist or suffer the dire consequences of non-compliance. Some of the Celestial Pures ignored the edict, while others became outright defiant.

Subsequently, Motherships were dispatched from the different home planets and eventually arrived at Earth's atmospheric door.

Battles between the Celestials took place all over the globe. Many, like those described in the **Mahabharata**, were chronicled by the Earthkind below.

In the end, the Celestials from the home planets prevailed and the offending Celestial Overseers were replaced by a new set of Celestial Pures who almost immediately set out to bend the will of the Mutes into submission, not through acts of violence or sadistic threats, but by promises of immortality via religion and the Divine reward of wealth and prosperity predicated upon blind, incontrovertible obedience.

It worked brilliantly, and still works today, although for the life of me, I don't understand why.

We, ladies and gentlemen, are the remnants of the offspring of the Celestial Pures who once ruled the skies. The descendants of the very Sky Gods Themselves and the Kings and Queens They sired. We are Their enduring legacy, and We are still manipulating this planet from behind the scenes. We are still the power behind the throne and We still revel in it as Our proverbial birthright, for We are the true "Remnants of Royalty".

Now, you will have to excuse me for a moment so that I might address some pressing matters at hand.

CHAPTER 2

END THE BEGINNING

Australia: If everyone has taken advantage of my time away to visit the facilities, then I would like to officially resume these proceedings.

Unfortunately, the news I have just received portends to be troubling at best. Our internal spy has just informed me that the militant branch of the Free Earth Society called the Free Earth Movement, which has been persistently trying to locate this precise location, has somehow successfully ascertained Our approximate whereabouts.

My inside source tells me that they have begun to move their assets and personnel in our general direction. As of now they know what building We are in, but not the actual floor or suite.

I suggest We get on with these proceedings, post haste, as he has assured me that they are still hours away from effectuating any serious disruption. As a precaution I have already put Our outside and inside security on heightened alert. After having rescanned this room I have detected a minor anomaly in the proximity of this window. Let me see…

Aha, here it is. A surveillance device disguised as a smoke alarm. I will have security remove it from this floor and plant it elsewhere so as to not alert them of Our discovery. Hopefully that will significantly deter their egress.

I will also have the lights significantly lowered so as to impede the surveillance of any hidden cameras We may not be aware of.

Shall We continue?

We are here to discuss matters of the utmost importance. No decision ever made compares to the one We have been tasked to make today. If You weren't all held in the highest esteem, You would not be in this room right now. This is not the time for levity or pettiness; it is rather the time for grave seriousness and sober contemplation. We are here to discuss the fate of the planet Earth and its inhabitants, which unfortunately also pertains to You and all of Your loved ones.

Those of You who have attended past Council of the Anunnaki Summits are accustomed to giving progress reports on the advancement of the now indigenous Human population. Today, however, We are here to make a determination as to the efficacy of Our continued involvement and protection of the Earth Human populace.

This "Eden Experiment" is about to end, one way or another. How and when will be up to Us, as this is officially the preordained conclusion of what was begun some 50,000-plus years ago.

We shall determine the guidelines for the "**Second Coming**" of Our Celestial brethren, as it has been written, foretold and prophesized since the beginning of this planet's Human seeding, by nearly every civilization on Earth, past and present; including The **Mayan Calendar, Nostradamus' End of the World predictions**, the Hopi's **Blue Kachina prophesy**, the Norse's **Ragnarok**, the **Apocalypse** of the **Dead Sea Scrolls** and the Christian Bible's **Armageddon** or **End Times**, to name a few.

We have been given four scenarios to choose from.

The first is **Eradication**.
This would call for the total extermination of all Human life on the planet Earth. This scenario suggests that the "Eden Experiment" here on Earth has been a dismal and abject failure.

The second is **Subjugation**.
This scenario calls for the total re-enslavement of Earth Humans for their own benefit, and for the benefit of the cosmos.

The third is **Emancipation**.
This scenario would prove preferable to the Free Earth Society, and would entail total desertion, a cessation of all observation and involvement, and an end to the subtle influence and manipulations currently engaged in on the part of Celestial and Earth Pures like Ourselves.

The fourth is **Edification**.
This last scenario entails a sharing of technological, agricultural, medicinal and spiritual guidance which would hopefully propel Earthkind into a brighter and far less perilous future.

At the end of Our discussions We shall take a vote, and a signal shall be dispatched that will instruct Our ancestral planets as to what Our agreed-upon course of action should be.

That decision must be based on a 60% or higher compliance, meaning that at least seven of Us must agree. We are mandated to remain here until an agreement has been reached, a vote has been taken, and the signal has been sent.

Representatives of each of the four ideologies are present.

Let Us discuss.

Unbeknownst to all of You, the twelve of Us have been carefully selected because of Our predispositions to align Ourselves with one or more of the aforementioned philosophical mind-sets.

Please correct me if I am in error.

Washington, Israel and Rome would align yourselves most closely with the Eradication scenario.

Washington: That is correct. I'd just as soon kill them all.

Israel: I don't harbor any hope for redemption, so I say let's exterminate them and start over.

Rome: I'd just as soon enslave them all, but I no longer believe We would ever accomplish a lasting compliance; and I have no intention of starting a never-ending war. So yes, eradication makes the most sense to me.

Australia: I have India, Peru, Russia and Ethiopia in the Subjugation camp.

India: I hate being shoved into boxes, but it is true that I would advocate the reinstitution of total control over the Mute population, in as much as they have repeatedly proven that they cannot effectively govern themselves.

Peru: You never waste a valuable asset just because it is flawed. You simply learn how to better exploit it to your needs and desires. Why pour out the wine just because the glass is chipped. Simply sip from the other side.

Russia: Wills can be broken. Order can be imposed. Wild horses can be tamed and rivers can be dammed. The unruly ways of the Mutes can be damned also.

Ethiopia: Of late, I have been reassessing my views on things. Where once I staunchly believed in beating the Mutes into submission, I now find my rhetoric has been softening and my tolerance growing. I am anxious to see where this discussion takes me.

Australia: Egypt and China, the Emancipation camp?

Egypt: Yeah, I guess so. I'm just tired of the whole "Why can't you people get it together?" crap. They're permanently screwed up, so We should just pack up Our stuff and leave them the hell alone, like We promised.

China: I believe in honoring an agreement, even if I find that it is no longer in my best interest to do so. If We go back on Our word, then doesn't that make Us just as immoral as they supposedly are?

Australia: Britain and Japan, the Edification camp, right?

Britain: Most assuredly. Once upon a time I would have said let's just leave, but now I honestly believe the Non-pures show genuine signs of spiritual and conscientious maturity. They just need a little "push" in the right direction, before it's too late.

Japan:	Are you kidding me? Non-pures would rock if We'd just kickstart them into the next phase of their development. We'd all benefit from their ascendance. Making their lives better would definitely make Our own lives demonstrably better.
Australia:	Thank you all. This may prove to be an intriguing if not dangerously daunting enterprise We are about to embark upon.
Egypt:	Wait a minute. What camp do you belong to? Where do you stand?
Australia:	Right dead in the middle.
Japan:	Four doesn't have a middle.
Australia:	Exactly. Persuade me.
	Let's have a discussion on where humanity is and where it has been.
Washington:	Where it has been… is in the sewer!
Most:	Civility!
Britain:	Well, I personally believe we have come quite a long way from the days of the unwashed **Druids** and the conscience-bereft barbarians that once roamed the Isles.
Egypt:	You wouldn't think so if you were surrounded by people constantly shouting for **Jihad** and engaging in unending provocations of conflict.
Russia:	That's what you get for not squashing the **Arab Spring** when you had the chance.
Egypt:	The Arab Spring was necessary to rid ourselves of the old ways and to try to find a new path into the future. But we have found that old ways die hard. People are prone to cling to what they know, even if they hate it.
Washington:	Well, you told us to stay the hell out of it, so we're gonna let you handle your own pathetic mess now.
Israel:	It's the same conflict that has gone on for centuries and shows little sign of abatement. A peace agreement is lucky if it outlives its scribes.
China:	I really don't understand why Human Beings can never seem to stop fighting.
India:	It is our nature to do so. Such as it has ever been and will ever be. Even now some of us unflinchingly hold on to a perverse desire to kill *everyone*.

Japan:	I don't think Mr. Washington *really* meant that.
Washington:	Think again, buddy. I meant it.
	I'm quite a bit older than you are, and I've fought in two wars. Mankind is one big steaming pile of shit.
Rome:	I agree. You're a fool if you think you can change Human nature. We love drama. We thrive on conflict and conquest. We always want to end up on top, and we're never satisfied, even when we get there.
	All Humans, even the Pure ones, have a need to feel like they're superior to someone else; and we're innately jealous of those who are more successful than ourselves.
	For Human Beings, there is no such thing as enough…only more. More money, more respect, more envy, more junk, more control, more power. More stuff we don't even need or want; just as long as it's more than somebody else has.
Peru:	Some of Us deserve more because We are worth more. My family employs thousands of people who feed their families with the money We pay them.
	My family is better educated, better-looking, better dressed, better prepared, and thusly better respected than the wretched masses around Us. They know it, and We know it.
Ethiopia:	And you will be sure to never let them forget it, not even for a moment. You find your self-worth in what you have, and not in what kind of a person you are inside. You believe the world owes you something because you were born privileged. You sound just like every other greedy little Mute millionaire.
Peru:	That's "billionaire" to you, Papi!
Israel:	What difference does it ultimately make? We rich people spend half of our time trying to make more money, and the other half worrying about who's trying to take it from us. That, my friends, is the new meaning of life. He who dies with the most…wins.
China:	Boy, what a pessimistic way of looking at life. Find your Zen, my friend.
India:	Where I come from, some Mutes believe that they were born poor because they are paying for a past debt to their Karma. What nonsense. Where do they come up with this stuff?
Ethiopia:	*We* gave a lot of it to them.

Japan:	Confusion is the workshop of the Devil. Oh, wait a minute, that would make Us the Devil!
Rome:	I'm glad you find this whole thing amusing. In a little while We'll be calling down the wrath of Heaven itself, perhaps in the shape of an asteroid, on these ill-prepared fools. We're going to finally put them out of their misery.
Egypt:	The misery We instigated? It's just not fair to punish them because they can't walk upright after We crippled them with the superstitious nonsense We put into their heads, or forced down their throats.
	We dared them to defy Us! We slaughtered them for their insolence. We beat them into bloody submission and condemned their souls to Hell for raising their eyes to Us with a questioning gaze. And now you want to finish the job We started, by breaking every promise We ever made to them? I guess I just don't know what it feels like to be a proud Pure anymore. And if We actually go through with this, I guess I never will!
Washington:	Aww, is the little baby going to cry?
	Why should you care what happens to these pathetic cretins? We're only expediting what they're sure to accomplish on their own, given time. Look at their nuclear weapons, global warming and abject hatred for one another. Hell, they slaughter each other all the time, just for the fun of it, or simply because they're "bored."
Egypt:	I'm not saying they're not brain-damaged. I'm just saying that most of their psychological damage was caused by Us.
India:	So, it's Our fault that they're too stupid to see the light and free themselves from the yoke of religion? They use religion to justify just about every level of inhumanity they can bestow upon each other.
	When is the last time you heard of a Celestial or Earth Pure threatening Mutes with Holy retribution?
Britain:	Today. And I weep. Not so much for them, but for how low We Ourselves have fallen.
Israel:	Fallen? Fallen? We've never been any better than We are right now. Have you forgotten how We Pures destroyed the planet of Our origin? Have you forgotten how We've routinely tried to destroy the people of this very planet by initiating wars, disease, floods, earthquakes, hurricanes, tsunamis, asteroid strikes, drought, volcanic eruptions and famine? Have you forgotten?
	This is nothing new to Us. It's just putting an end to the madness We created.

We *owe* it to them to end them.

Ethiopia: Stop it, stop it, stop it!

What the Hell is wrong with some of You? They are Us and We are them! Would you kill your own mother because she disappointed you? Are We really ready to live with the fact that We are mass murderers? Are We truly no more enlightened than our Non-pure brethren?

I am not sure that I could live with myself.

Rome: So, you like living in this cesspool?

Ethiopia: If it is a cesspool, then We are wading in Our own shit.

Japan: But it doesn't have to be this way. We can make things better by helping *them* be better.

A starving man will steal to survive. But if he is well fed he sees no need to steal. A drowning man will clutch at straws, so why not throw him a life preserver, or better still, pull him into the boat?

By slowly bringing the Non-pures out of the dark and into the light of the truth, We can guide them towards a better world free from prejudice, envy and selfishness.

Peru: What's in it for me?

Britain: Why does it always have to be about you?

Peru: Good question. Maybe because it *is*.

Russia: Ignore her.

Peru: Go to Hell!

Russia: Are you inviting me over? But, what will your concubine of a husband say?

All: Civility!

Australia: Am I going to have to knock both of you out?

Peru: If you do, start running and never look back.

India: Like Russia said, ignore her. And Peru, unless you think you'd enjoy suddenly going blind, I would advise you to put your eyes back in your head.

When you start acting like a Pure, We'll start treating you like one.

Peru: Oh, but you are mistaken. I **am** acting like a Pure. It is you who is starting to sound and smell like a Tainted Mute! Where is your Pure pride?

India: What do you know about pride, you *suuang...bot* whore!

Australia: Ladies! And I use the term loosely. We are here to discuss the end of this world as We know it, and the two of you want to argue about who has the bigger shoe size. Really?

India: I apologize for my inappropriate language and for the loss of my composure. It will not happen again.

Peru: See that it doesn't.

Egypt: I would have bet my life that Peru wasn't going to also apologize. And I would have won a fortune.

Japan: I'm with Washington now. Kill them all… and Us with them.

I have a horrible headache!

Ethiopia: I do too. And I never get headaches. Are you sure it isn't your tech that's causing this, Mr. Chairman?

Australia: I'm positive. But I think there may be another source of a transmission in this room.

For now, let Us continue. Let Us try a more civil and organized approach.

And can We please try to eliminate the profanity and personal attacks altogether?

All: Agreed.

Australia: Very well then. Let's discuss racial bias.

Britain: Ours or theirs?

Israel: Surely you don't believe that We Pures harbor any racial bias? I don't believe that anyone in this room even notices the color of another man's skin, except to compliment a nice tan.

China: Mute, Taint, Dim, Half-Breed, Mental Midget? Really? No biases?

Israel:	That's different.
China:	Why, because you say so?
	When you criticize a person for something they can't change, or for circumstances they're in that they had nothing to do with creating, then isn't it ultimately exactly the same? A Non-pure can't change his mental status any more than you can change your race. He or she is just playing the hand life has dealt them.
Peru:	And I am just playing the hand that life has dealt me. I can't help it if I was born a winner, while others were born losers. They don't feel sorry for me and I sure as hell don't feel sorry for them. We can't all be rich and beautiful. If we were, then being rich and beautiful would mean nothing. You'd just be average. And I will *never* be average.
Ethiopia:	And when you die, will you not find yourself average then? Your soul will be no more special than anyone else's. Unless of course the myths are true and your corrupted spirit is sent to Hell.
Peru:	Listening to your voice is all the Hell I ever expect to endure.
India:	I believe we create our own Heaven and Hell out of our expectations. If we are good people, the afterlife, if there is one, will give us what we truly believe we deserve. But you cannot fool yourself, only others. Being a nasty, selfish Human Being eats at your soul, and you will condemn yourself to a miserable afterlife where your self-recriminations will haunt you forever.
Russia:	I don't know where you got that from, but I am going to use it! That is, if We're still here.
Rome:	You just might have something there. Self-exoneration or condemnation. That really gives me something to think about.
	Okay, I'm in the Emancipation camp now! I can feel my Karma purifying as We speak.
India:	Don't make fun. It doesn't become you.
Rome:	Actually, I'm being dead serious. I know I spout off at the mouth without considering my words very often, but I live in the Vatican because I take this transmigration of the soul thing very seriously.
	I just know for a fact that what they're selling in there, with all of their pomp and circumstance, is not the truth. And sadly enough, so do they.

I'm pretty sure the soul continues on, and so I've spent a lifetime trying to figure out the truth about exactly where it goes and what happens when it gets there.

Ethiopia: I have been on the same path lately, my brother. And I fear that the decision We are here to make will either condemn Us or free Us forever. No matter what We decide, We cannot allow Our subconscious biases to take Us down the wrong path.

Do I kill the sleeping lion while I have the chance, or do I wait to see if it will attack and destroy me and my family? In which case, it may be too late.

Japan: I agree wholeheartedly. Helping Non-pures may or may not be the right thing to do in the long run, but not giving them the chance to save themselves says more about who We are than it does about them.

If you tame and befriend the lion, then he may in turn save your life one day when the hyenas attack.

Washington: Okay, enough with the Lion King allusions. I get your point. Despite the general consensus, I am a reasonable guy at heart. But I am also a pragmatist.

You know, I must admit that there was a time when I didn't like Blacks, or Mexicans, or Arabs, or Indians, homegrown or foreign, or Asians, or White folks. And then I realized that that time was *here* and *now*.

I'm an equal opportunity hater.

And I learned something else today; that I hate You damn Pures too! All of You get on my last nerve!

In fairness, maybe I need to ask myself one very important question. Is it really *You* who are all screwed up, or is it *me*? And the answer is….. drum roll please….. It's YOU!

Human Beings are just the pits. They whine all the time and bitch and moan about every little thing.

Britain: You mean, like you're doing right now?

Washington: Yeah, maybe. But I've earned the right to hate humanity.

Australia: How so….no pun intended.

Washington: Sure. Humans can't help but hate one another. We're just so… hateable.

Once in a while I sit and contemplate about how different my world would be if Europeans had just stayed on their side of the world and left the Americas alone. Instead they intruded on our land, bringing diseases and weapons the likes of which we'd never seen, and a wanton hatred and disregard for anyone with skin that was darker than their own.

They called us savages because we fought for what was ours. They raped our women, our culture and the landscape, all at the same time. Our preemptive strikes were called brutal massacres while theirs were justified as "necessary" security measures. They incarcerated us and spat upon our customs, beliefs and way of life.

Racial bias? Yeah, I've got some racial bias for you.

The Incas, Mayans and Aztecs were building monuments the whole world is still in awe of today, until they were slaughtered by the greedy, soulless Conquistadors and their ilk. Missionaries followed up and turned the little red and brown "savages" into basket weavers. We've never fully recovered from their systematic ethnic and cultural degradation.

Japan: We sit here and discuss whether or not extinction is an option. When they dropped the nuclear bombs on **Hiroshima** and **Nagasaki**, that question was answered forever.

We knew they had the bomb, and we knew they were willing to use it on us, and so **Pearl Harbor** was our preemptive strike. Of course, they predictively refused to see it that way.

Little yellow slant-eyed men, women and children deserved to be callously wiped off the face of the Earth, with no lingering remorse or guilt-ridden regret. They decided that the wholesale slaughter of innocent Japanese civilians was both justified and "necessary" to achieve an expedient means to an already predictable end. Or maybe they just wanted to see just how much damage their merciless bomb could do.

Israel: As if hundreds of years of Egyptian slavery were not enough, the Romans walked in and beat my people into submission. They taxed us, put their foot on our Hebrew necks, and dared us to resist in any way. We meant less than nothing to them. And so we bequeathed them a conscience in the guise of Christianity.

That worked for a while, until we found ourselves being systematically expelled from virtually every other country in the world. They rounded us up, turned on the gas, and threw the hook-nosed, curly-headed bodies of the little Jewish immigrants into the ovens. A proper burial was too good for us. After all, look at what we'd done to them. We had swept their streets, baked their bread, made their shoes, and kissed their asses.

And look what it got us. But then, our extermination was deemed "necessary" to cleanse the white race.

And so, having learned the lessons of undeserved hatred the world had so brutally beaten into us, we returned home to Israel. And we haven't known peace since.

Racial bias. What is that? Can We now justify killing **billions** of innocent women and children? You tell me.

Ethiopia: The only good black man… is a dead black man. At least that's the message my continent has bought into.

Tribal hatred knows no bounds. No amount of killing and mutilation is too great. Rape is a form of genocide because the baby's blood will not be pure, and who will ever want to marry the damaged and spiritually mutilated women we leave behind us?

Angola, Rwanda, Sudan, South Africa, Uganda, Somalia, the Democratic Republic of Congo, Nigeria, Sierra Leone, Ethiopia, and numerous other African nations have attempted to systematically exterminate the people of their own countries.

We don't need white Europeans to tell us that black lives are worthless. We tell *them* every day as black men slaughter each other in the streets. As we hack each other to pieces with machetes. As we hand the guns to our children and tell them to kill. Because for them to ever know peace… killing other black people is unavoidably "necessary."

India: You would be a Dalit in my country. An Untouchable. You would be destined to beg in the streets and pick through garbage from the day you were born, and no person of any stature would ever marry you. You would be Indian through and through, but you would be looked down upon because of your lowly heritage.

Once upon a time we fought over religious matters. We hated each other enough to separate into two different countries, after nearly two million of us died due to religiously inspired violence. And to this day, distrust based on religious ideology continues to separate us.

And I am sure that the day will come that we will use the bomb on each other, because changing minds is tantamount to changing hearts, and we have forgotten who and what we were meant to be. Now there is only hatred and bitterness where understanding and tolerance used to live.

They may look like us, but don't you dare call me "one of those."

Will our ethnic and religious biases ultimately drive us to exterminate one another? Only if we deem it "necessary."

Peru: I have no idea what any of you are talking about.

The millions of people who live in the slums of South American cities live there by choice. They are comfortable in each other's filth, and have grown 100 percent accustomed to their wretched circumstances. They are societally "shop blind," meaning that they no longer see, smell, taste, or are repulsed by the deplorable conditions in which they live. It has become their acceptable way of life. They are worthless and disgusting.

They grow and sell drugs because they have convinced themselves that it is a legitimate occupation. Corruption is expected and blatant political lies are cheered and applauded. Everyone turns their backs and ignores the wholesale slaughter of those who inadvertently cross the paths of the sadistic drug lords and street gangs. Headless bodies are a clear message that everyone understands. Kidnapping is a lucrative and viable enterprise.

Dealing death is once again an acceptable way of life.

The **Street Children of South America** have become an embarrassment and a nuisance, and I am glad there are those who are willing to reduce the numbers of these little uneducated beggars and thieves before they overwhelm us. Their culling is both prudent and "necessary."

It isn't racial bias; it is a socioeconomic divide that grows ever deeper.

And yes, we all hate Argentineans… because *they are* racists and they know it. After all, they killed off virtually all of their indigenous population. Poor little Indians. See… I have a heart.

Rome: Is it a racial bias to believe you are better than everybody else, if it's true?

Rome practically conquered the whole world! We marched across continents, systematically eliminating inferior races. We put everyone in their proper place… which is beneath us. We cared for no one but ourselves as we callously spread our superior culture out across the world. We were the self-proclaimed cradle of civilization. Slaughtering other races and civilizations was our birthright. It was "Our way, or death… you choose." It was us… and everybody else. Bloodshed was deemed a "necessity"; an easily replicable means to an end.

Britain: At least *we* were polite about it. I don't think we ever realized that we had any blood on our hands. Maybe that's why we wore gloves.

No other culture on Earth was seen to be as regally dignified and altruistically intentioned. Not the Romans, not the Spaniards, and certainly not the French.

We convinced ourselves that we were doing the world a favor as we mowed down hundreds of thousands of ungrateful dirt-eating savages led by uncouth, unsophisticated and unappreciative would-be kings.

We were convinced that the whole world would thank us one day for bringing their ignorant, backward, unkempt asses out of the primeval dark and into the light of reasoned civilized day.

The more people we killed, the more the world understood that destiny had placed us at their grimy doorsteps, and that a more refined existence was beckoning them to answer our bloody knock.

God-ordained and King- or Queen-advocated violence was "necessary", because it was the only language most of the inferior wretches could understand.

Russia: We tried. We were surrounded by disorganized ignoramuses who were never going to amount to anything on their own. We tried to show them that there is strength in numbers. And eventually we realized that a supreme show of force would be deemed "necessary" to achieve our global aspirations. So we systematically beat them senseless and encouraged them to, willingly or unwillingly, join our little global fight club.

Why be a pathetic nobody of a country when you could be a card-carrying member of the U.S.S.R.? Why not rule the world with us? We only killed them to show them how inexorably powerful we were. In return, we were willing to unhesitatingly bash in the skulls of any brazen enemies who might happen to threaten them. So, why would any sane country reject such an offer?

They should have felt honored that Russians were even willing to sit at the same table with their weak, ugly asses.

But I don't see where racial bias entered into it. It was more like a lopsided, exploitative business alliance, in which we insisted on maintaining the upper hand at all times.

Threatening to blow people up got old after a while, and one day we were told to put up or shut up. So, we shut up and disbanded the Union. Killing for profit makes sense, but killing for power garners respect.

After all, what's a little World War among friends?

China: So, you wanted to rule the world by any means necessary? Well, we believed in the closed door policy. We didn't want the world watching our internal struggles, which culminated with the Communist Party ultimately uniting us into the People's Republic of China. Eight million casualties of war seemed like a very "necessary" and reasonable loss.

Consequently, Japan and Taiwan learned not to mess with us.

Why couldn't Korea, Vietnam, and Burma see the light like Tibet?

Racial bias is reserved for the disdain we hold for the rest of the entire world.

We don't like or respect any of you. We outnumber you. We tolerate you, and someday we will own you. Have a nice day.

Egypt: You won't own us, because we own the oil!

At this very moment we are gouging the entire planet to get even for the centuries of abuse we suffered from your endless escapades across our barren borders.

We have never earned your respect, and killing an Arab has always been an acceptable and inconsequential thing to do. You all thought you were Lawrence of Arabia, and had given yourselves the right to exploit the Arab world in any way you saw fit. Until we stood up and declared that enough was enough.

We have shown you that we are willing to die to preserve what we believe in. We are even willing to kill the innocent women and children of our very own countries, if "necessary," to show them that mingling with the **Infidels** is tantamount to religious treason.

At this very moment we are slaughtering each other over some unknown nebulous concept of a caliphate nation that is both democratic and Islamic.

Why should Muslims fight and kill you, when we can fight and kill each other?

I'm not really sure what racial bias is. Everybody hates Arabs, and we hate all non-Muslims. The color of your skin or your nationality has little to do with it.

We would rather destroy the world, than to question our Islamic values.

Australia: I'm sure that most of you see Australians as weak, unassuming, peaceful and unprovocative. And you would be correct.

We don't worry about race, and race doesn't worry about us, so come on down!

Ethiopia: What about the **Aborigines?**

Australia: What about us, Mate? We're happy and well fed. They take care of us. They employ us without hesitation and for the most part leave us alone.

I mean, it's true that they forced most of us to become Christians, but then, that was for our own aggrandizement. And the **Aboriginal Reserves, Stations** and **Missions** were a sensible solution to a complex problem.

They got rid of racism in the **1967 referendum**. They simply scribbled out all of the old distinctions they'd always made between **quadroons, half-caste,** and **full-blooded**. That made everything hunky dory. Heck, they even started allowing us to vote! Just ask any white Australian if their collective conscience isn't a lot clearer now.

Hell, now Aborigines can even marry without the white man's permission! We've come a long way, baby! Some of us straighten and lighten our hair to appear more European, no matter how preposterous it looks.

Many of us would just as soon drink ourselves to death before we assimilate.

But, we've been told that we have nice teeth!

We'll never be them, and they like it that way. We own nothing of consequence, and are stuck somewhere between feelings of pride and self-hatred. They outlive us by 20 years. We have 6 times the suicide rate and 4 times the unemployment rate.

We may be the oldest civilization on Earth, but they found it "necessary" to slaughter us for being audacious enough to fight for our own land as they stole it from us.

And later to add insult to injury, they deemed it "necessary" to take away our children and house them in "missions" because they unilaterally decided that we were "unfit" to raise them.

After initially declaring the continent of Australia to be **"uninhabited by humans,"** the white settler population watched as the Aboriginal population shrank from an estimated 300,000 when they arrived, to approximately 60,000 today.

But there is no racism on the continent of Australia; only elitism and unwarranted pride. After all, you can't truly help a people who don't want your stinkin' help, can you?

Japan: Wow.

Australia: So, as we have all willingly admitted, killing Non-pures has never been taboo. They've been slaughtered "for their own good" for 50,000 years. Both We and they have wiped out civilization after civilization in a futile attempt to bring order to the chaos that is humanity.

The Eradication scenario would simply put a final exclamation point on a universally accepted tradition of rationalized genocidal behavior.

CHAPTER 3

THE RELIGION AGENDA

Australia:	Pack it up, ladies and gentlemen. We are moving to a more secure location.
Russia:	Why, what happened?
Australia:	It appears I was right. There is another transmitter in this room.
	I will scan you one at a time and dismiss you to wait by the door with security until We have all been cleared.
India:	Is this really necessary? I don't believe anyone here is a spy. I have been doing some scanning myself, while everyone thought I was meditating.
Australia:	I understand. But my source has just informed me that the Free Earth Movement operatives know exactly where We are. He even gave me this suite number. Mr. Russia, please rise.
Russia:	Very well, just don't put your hands on me.
Australia:	Please wait by the door. Ms. Britain, you're next.
Britain:	Let me know if you find anything you like.
Australia:	Please hold your cape open for me. Okay, you're clear.
Britain:	Aren't you going to frisk me? I might have something hidden in my undergarments.
Australia:	Mr. Washington, please rise. Okay, you're good to go. Please wait over there, and don't forget your notepad.
Washington:	Ms. Britain, I have something I want to ask you!
Britain:	Send me an email.
Australia:	Ms. Peru, you're next.
Peru:	Don't even *try* to frisk me. Can I go?
Australia:	Hold on a second, Ms. Peru. Please remove your necklace.

Peru:	Why? I told you it was a gift from my husband this morning.
Australia:	Yes, and it also has a transmitter integrated into its design. I'm sorry but I'm going to have to confiscate it, and it will be left in this room as a decoy.
Russia:	I knew that bitch was the spy!
Washington:	Let me take her traitorous little head off.
Japan:	I'd like to have that honor myself. I promise, it will be almost painless.

(Against her will, Peru slowly begins to rise above the floor with her arms and legs awkwardly outstretched to either side.)

Peru:	Wait, I swear to you I am not a spy! I swear it! Let me down at once!
Australia:	Back off, everyone, she's telling the truth!
China:	How can she be telling the truth? You clearly found the transmitter in her possession. We were all witnesses.
Australia:	Those of you with heightened telepathy can confirm that Ms. Peru is not lying, and did not know that she was in possession of the transmitter.
India:	He's right. Let her down. She didn't know she had it on her. If she was lying, I'd know.

(Abruptly, Peru crashes to the floor and quickly leaps to her feet.)

Australia.	I will immediately launch an investigation into the whereabouts of her husband and into any recent contacts he has made.
Peru:	The next time one of you heathens chooses to put your mind on me, I won't be so forgiving.
	Mr. Chairman, I promise you, my husband is not a spy. But I can't vouch for his jeweler. Have him checked out. Can't you remove the transmitter and let me keep the necklace? It's so lovely.
Australia:	There's no time, and if I break the transmitter while trying to remove it, it may alert them that we're on to them. If they discover we've been tipped off, it may inadvertently expose my inside man, and I can't permit that to happen.
Peru:	What a shame. I'll just have to have another one made.

Australia:	By the door, Ms. Peru. Don't forget your coffee.
	You're clear too, Ms. India.
	Mr. Japan, you're clear.
	Mr. China, you're clear also.
	Hold on, Mr. Israel. What's that? (Australia asked, pointing at his chest.)
Israel:	A pacemaker. Thanks for bringing it to everyone's attention.
Australia:	I had to ask, even though I already knew. I wanted to measure your response ratios. You're good.
	Rome, you're clear.
	And, Mr. Egypt, you...are...clear.
	Mr. Ethiopia, please raise your arms. Thank you, you're clear. Don't forget your briefcase.
Ethiopia:	Was I just relegated to the back of your metaphorical bus?
Australia:	Not intentionally. I just wanted you to remain here with me in case we encountered any more problems. You know, as backup.
Ethiopia:	A very wise answer. I am starting to like you.
Australia:	Excellent! I need you all to follow security to Our new location where I will meet you after I've retrieved the transcorder.
Britain:	See you there!

Seven minutes later.

Russia:	This place is like a bunker.
Washington:	I know what you mean. Look how thick the doors are.
Australia:	I see that all of you have seemingly made yourselves comfortable and have realigned my seating arrangement. Unfortunately, I need you to take a seat in the same proximity to each other as you were occupying upstairs.
Rome:	Why? I want to sit next to Ms. Britain.

Britain:	Trust me, it won't do you any good. Just move.
Japan:	I'm not comfortable sitting across from Ms. Peru. She keeps giving me dirty looks.
Peru:	And you wouldn't know that, if you'd stop staring at me and licking your lips.
Egypt:	Busted!
Japan:	Whatevvver! Trade seats with me.
Australia:	All right, if we're all relatively comfortable, let's begin. The new topic is religion.
Rome:	Oh boy. Do we have to?
Australia:	Yes. If we are going to make an informed decision, we need to thoroughly discuss all of the determining factors. Religion drives 50% of the world's conflicts and 60% of its behavior. Religion is a primary catalyst for both peace and revolution. Religion is a staple in most Non-pure's lives. Religion is the opiate of the world; its most prevalent pacifier, as well as its foremost stimulant for aggression. People will kill for it, die for it, live for it, and despise it. Religion keeps them awake at night and lulls them to sleep with reassurances of a God-protected slumber. Religion is the ultimate false sense of security. Religion is nonsense clad in regal attire. It is mysticism posing as certainty; deception in the guise of devoutness. Religion motivates people to reach out to others as it simultaneously builds walls between them. Religion tells them to love while teaching them to distrust and to hate one another. It turns warriors into pacifists and good men into homicidal zealots. Religion unites while dividing. It meshes supposition with lies. It informs as it deceives. It makes man both loving and intolerant.

Religion demands allegiance as it hand-delivers alienation.

Religion defines righteous behavior as it confirms one's inalienable, sinful nature. It teaches forgiveness as it preaches eternal punishment for noncompliance.

Religion entices you with Heaven as it threatens you with Hell. It soothes and it frightens. It is, at once, freeing and burdensome.

Religion encourages prayer but delivers little more than unreliable happenstance.

Religion is a roadmap to incomprehensibility.

Religion fabricates mankind's beginning, while prophesying mankind's end. It professes to explain the world's creation, while immersing itself in mythos. It exudes wisdom as it exposes its ignorance. It sidesteps reasonable questions as it beseeches faith.

Religion implores obedience and yet indiscriminately forgives repeated indiscretions.

Religion is the truth buried in lies; confusion, wrapped in hope.

Religion is the problem that insists it's the solution. A disease that is promoted as a cure.

Religion… is the topic of our conversation.

Japan: I am scared of you!

Britain: Let me catch my breath.

Russia: Did you make that up by yourself?

Ethiopia: Sir, you have been touched by the Divine.

Rome: I want a recording of that.

Australia: Thank you.

Religion has a twin brother named **Superstition**. At times it seems impossible to tell them apart. They tend to sound so much alike that we are oftentimes confused as to which one is speaking.

Instead of insisting that they are one and the same, and asking that age-old question as to whether or not one has ever seen them together at the same time, why not ask if one has, instead, ever seen them apart?

Members of every religious ideology profess to being able to tell one from the other, but those outside of that religion would be quick to insist that much, if not most, of another's religion is nonsensical conjecture based upon unrealistic, superstitiously based mythos.

Humankind has ever sought answers to life's biggest questions. Every person contemplates the afterlife and wonders if it is indeed the end of everything, or immortality, that looms in their future. And who can blame them?

We all seek confirmable answers and reassurances.

We all seek certainty, but have decided that a well-lubricated lie will do.

We all want this life to mean something other than the obvious pain, struggle and inevitable atrophy. We all want death to be a new beginning rather than a pointless ending. We all "think" we want immortality; and that is precisely what religion promises us.

Whether it is Heaven, Nirvana, Reincarnation, or Valhalla, we all want to know if there is something and/or someone graciously awaiting us on the other side. After all, Heaven would be Hell without company. We are social beings by nature, and it has been proven that loneliness is oftentimes a stairway to insanity.

So, is it any wonder that Humankind desperately clings to their respective beliefs? Faced with the emptiness of oblivion, is it not better to gild oneself in the armor of faith?

Let us be honest. Given the alternative, what do they have to lose? If their religious beliefs prove to be true, then their faith will be gloriously rewarded, and if they prove to be false, we all may well remain obliviously unaware.

And so they hedge their bets. They profess to believe, but routinely behave as if they don't, so as to not let religion rob them of enjoying their lives. They all know that divine forgiveness is the proverbial back door to salvation; and that repeated acts of deliberate insubordination are not irredeemably fatal.

Isn't it their obligation to themselves to invest in the eternal-life insurance policy of a religion, with hopes that the company they are sending their premiums to is not, in fact, a shell corporation? Empty and bankrupt? Organized and run by charlatans and conmen? Part of them either knows or believes this to be true, while part of them stays busy drowning out and stifling their intrinsic common sense and protesting rationality.

Many profess to just not being smart enough or wise enough to sort through the hodgepodge of conflicting detritus called alternative faith; and so they opt to hitch their wagons to the local or most convenient star they see, knowing deep down inside that that star may in fact only be a moon which generates no light or heat of its own, and instead is sustained solely by the intransigence of their beliefs, rather than the power of its own validity.

And if, in fact, that is true, most of them would rather not know. They would prefer to live the lie rather than to stare uncertainty in the face. Profound ignorance is indeed bliss.

Or is it? Wouldn't we all rather know the truth, even if it exposes our current beliefs as being ill-informed and contrived; if that "antitruth" offered us an equally enriching alternative?

In other words, finding out that your abusive alcoholic father is *not,* in fact, your biological father, but that the philanthropic billionaire around the corner *is,* would only hurt momentarily until reality sets in and the promise of a better future suddenly is made manifest as your true father lovingly embraces you and welcomes you into his family.

As Human Beings we are predisposed to fear the unknown, but most fear can be overcome with bravery and resolve. Humankind would still live in caves and remain simple hunters and gatherers had we not taken chances and trusted in innovation and embraced change.

Perhaps it is time for mankind to cast off the superstitiously based and oftentimes illogically adhered-to traditions we have inherited, and willfully embrace brotherhood and the commonality that exists between us. We all inherently want exactly the same things in life. My innate propensity to envy you of yours will quickly dissipate when I take possession of my own.

Despite what some would have you believe, the "My religion is better than your religion." insanity that has been so pervasive on this planet, can eventually give way to a more reasoned and rational shared belief system, if one is enticingly proffered. History has repeatedly shown us this.

We Pures, as a rule, believe that the spirit/soul vacates the body at the moment of true death, but even We are left with question marks when We seek to precisely chart its journey forward. And so, even We form unsubstantiated beliefs based on hopes and desires. We are, after all, only Human Beings; and Our indefatigable will to survive will still override Our intellects when Our inherent insecurities are properly provoked.

So, how do We sort it all out? How do We decide whether or not to squash religiosity or to further manipulate it? Let Us look at present-day religions and see if We might come to a better understanding as to how they came to be what they are today; and attempt to surmise from that what the Celestial Pures of the past sought to achieve.

First of all, let Us remind Ourselves that the First Drops were well aware of who they were and where they came from. But without the technology of the Celestial Pures above, and without pencils, paper, or recording devices, their knowledge was usually passed down to future generations of Earthborn Non-pures via an oral tradition.

Some attempted to relay information on cave walls with paintings or by carving their histories into stone. But the truth will always be clouded and mangled by interpretation. And without the original orators to confirm, deny or explain what they were trying to convey, conjecture and misinterpretation reared their collective heads and sprayed the graffiti of superstition and illogic all over their encrypted artwork, leaving it understandably indiscernible and oftentimes incomprehensible.

Let us also remember that thousands of years had passed between the time of the initial Drops and the Celestial promulgation of most of the new religions. Populations had grown from hundreds to multiples of thousands. Civilizations had already taken root, and primitive religions and belief systems had already become manifest.

Celestial Pures were faced with trying to comprehend belief traditions that were so incongruent with anything They had ever even considered, that the idea of morphing those beliefs and traditions into something more coherent and exploitable was a daunting task at best.

The Aboriginal people of Australia, for example, have a religion that is steeped in mysticism and ritual.

Outsiders have little to no chance of ever adequately comprehending or accurately explaining the underpinnings of the **Dreamtime Stories**. The fact that all of nature is an **anthropomorphic** construct, based on **animism**, tells us that their entire world is alive and imbued with a soul. This includes rocks, vegetation, animals and even the hillsides themselves.

Baiame, a Celestial Overseer, found that He was looked upon as the Creator God or Sky Father, long after His involvement with the Aboriginals had begun. Despite His efforts to assure them otherwise, His denials were deemed humility, and the fact that He had rerouted rivers, given them their laws and inspired their sacred traditions, songs and culture, reinforced their belief in Him. He was also falsely attributed with clearing patches of land for their **bora** or initiation sites where their boys are initiated into manhood.

In a last-ditch effort, Baiame forbade them to mention or discuss His name publicly, and He returned to the sky. But the damage was already done. The people could not deny what they had incomprehensibly observed, and so, could not be deterred from their burgeoning belief system.

The Aborigines had witnessed Baiame, and later the few local Earth Pures He left behind Him, move objects like rocks, dead tree branches and piles of leaves or debris with Their minds. What they were witnessing was **telekinesis**, but what they said was "He spoke to the rocks, and the rocks obeyed Him." This was interpreted by the people as those objects having a life or soul of their own.

You can't unring the bell. They had seen what they had seen, and thus the world itself was alive with purpose and intent. All things were connected and conscious. And the die of irrationality had been permanently cast.

All of life is like a dream as told in the **songlines** or **dreaming tracks** of their traditions that provide them with directions and speak of landmarks along the way. In other words, it works for them, even if the foundations of those beliefs are badly flawed and misinterpreted.

And thusly, are most religions born.

Peru: I love it! Celestials were afforded wonderful privileges back then. I wish They would permit Us to do those things now. They tell me I can't even move this coffee cup across the table in the presence of Mutes. Of course, once in a while I'll move one of *their* cups just an inch or two to watch their reactions!

Britain: You do that too! I love how excited they get when something seems to move on its own. It freaks them out!

Australia: Might I remind everyone that this Summit is being recorded.

Peru: Oops. Well, perhaps I can redeem myself by talking about a few crazy religions that once flourished in my neighborhood.

Australia: Sure. Proceed.

Peru: Human sacrifice. Need I say more?

Of course it didn't start out that way.

A **new** batch of Celestials arrived and found that agrarian societies had developed all over the region. Their predecessors like **Quetzalcoatl, Hunab Ku, Huitzilopochtli,** and **Viracocha** had done a fairly good job of making the Mutes self-sustainable; but the new Celestials like **Tezcatlipoca**, the twins **Hunahpu** and **Xbalanque, Tlaloc,** and later, Viracocha's son, Peru's beloved **Pachacuti,** decided to "kick" their respective civilizations into high gear.

First they installed Themselves, Their offspring, or other selected Earth Pures as Kings in the different colonies. These individuals were in direct telepathic communication with the "Sky Gods" above, and emphatically instructed the Mutes as to what they were required to do.

Using a few tools loaned to them by the Celestials, and at the direction of their divinely inspired Kings, they began building additional pyramids everywhere. Several of the "Gods" got into a contest and commissioned thousands of these temples to be built.

The **Olmec, Toltec, Maya, Aztec,** and **Inca** cultures all thrived under the Rule of the "Gods" who made the clouds rain, the rivers flow and the maize grow.

Elaborate artwork and artifacts were created, like the **Mayan Calendar,**

which beckons in the **Fifth age of humanity**, during which catastrophic life-ending events will occur that will culminate with mankind realizing its spiritual destiny.

This will be followed by the **Sixth age**, where mankind will realize God within themselves, and the **Seventh age**, where Mutes will once again become telepathic. Or so it is written.

Most of these empires consisted of a collection of different tribes that were patched together by the Gods Themselves to form vast civilizations.

Ceremonial opulence was evidence enough to convince the people that they were truly special in the eyes of the Gods, and that they would indeed be considered a part of something epic and monumental when the history of mankind on Earth was written.

Unfortunately, supreme power begets supreme ego, and the Celestials turned praiseworthy successes into extreme avarice and abusive indulgences. War became the norm, conquest a hobby, and ultimately, cannibalism a pastime.

The Mutes would do anything to please their Gods. No atrocity was too heinous and no sacrifice too unreasonable.

Apparently, word of these atrocities got back to the home planets, and the Cease-and-Desist Edict was issued.

After their Sky Gods were summarily deported during the Great Departure, the remaining Earth hierarchy of the region sought to continue the practices of the past by feigning communication with the now absent Powers up above.

Ceremonies and rituals no longer garnered the expected responses. The rain could no longer be beckoned at will. The crops began to shrivel and the people began to rebel against the harsh reign of their kings, who had grown desperate to maintain order.

And slowly but surely the people began to walk away. They abandoned their temples, killed or deposed their rulers, and fell to the invading forces from beyond the sea, who were often mistaken for the exiled Gods who had abandoned them.

Those Gods haven't returned to this day, and Their substantial accomplishments were surrendered to the voracious forests. The mighty Gods had truly fallen and along with Them, Their laudable legacies.

I'm sure there's a prescient lesson in there somewhere, but I just can't seem to find it.

Australia: Excellent, Ms. Peru. Would anyone else like to share a bit of local history?

China: Boy, do we have Gods!

During approximately the same era Ms. Peru was speaking of, our Celestial "Overlords" also lost Their collective minds. They sought to enslave the Chinese people and to subvert the already established religions of the region. However, They were not as successful, and Their efforts were eventually thwarted in the Great Alien War.

What these *new* Celestials found when They got to the planet Earth was that the "**Jade-Emperor**"—who ruled Heaven, mankind on Earth and Hell, at the behest of the **Three Pure Ones, Yuan-shi tian-zong**, also known as **Jade Pure** or the Perfect One, along with **Ling-Bao Tian-Song** or the **High Pure** and **Lao-jun** the **Supreme Pure**—had honored the Covenant that had brought the Non-pures to Earth.

How this Celestial Pure, the Jade Emperor, was portrayed, understood and deified, is mind-boggling. Somehow an encounter with the previously made-of-stone **Monkey King, Sun Wukong,** who the **Jade Emperor** invited to Heaven…

Why are you all looking at me that way? I didn't make all this stuff up. They still have festivals in His name. The Monkey King helped lead the cruel Celestials who enslaved us and forced us to build the now covered pyramids..... never mind.

Anyway, the Buddha sealed the Monkey King in a mountain, and later He was granted Buddhahood.

I give up. That was a book made into a cartoon. The point is, how many religions would ever allow a monkey to fight and repeatedly humiliate and defeat their most powerful Gods?

Chinese religion is an amalgamation of so many overlapping, mind-numbing, mythological, incomprehensible, nonsensical, headache-inducing paradoxes, that no sane man can explain it all to anyone's satisfaction.

You'd think by now that we would have just chucked the whole thing and moved on, but instead we keep incorporating all the newer religions into the old ones, or vice versa.

The Jade Emperor, who was a real live Celestial Pure, helped the Chinese Non-pures develop a vast civilization on Earth. He did this in a bureaucratic way by appointing lesser ranked Celestials and Earth Pures as Civil Servants to protect and monitor the behavior of every man, woman and child and report back to Him. These domestic Pures were also respected and prayed to regularly.

The Jade Emperor rewards or punishes each household according to the yearly reports He is given. However, individuals may attempt to bribe the lower Gods with gifts and such, to perhaps influence a more favorable report.

A Human may be deified and given the elixir of immortality for exceptional deeds performed on the part of mankind. Much like Catholic saints.

And then there are the **Eight Immortals...** whom I won't go into.

Think of Taoism (Daoism), whose founder **Zhuang Zhou** was an eccentric Earth Pure, **Buddhism** and **Confucianism,** as being philosophies and cultural practices instead of solely as religions. And they are all flexible enough to incorporate ethnic religions like that of the **Hans** into them.

It's amazing how easily Non-pures will accept and worship anything and everything they themselves deem sacred. I don't just mean other Humans, but also trees, rocks, mountains, caves, rivers... you name it.

Celestials manipulated them, in part, just because it was so easy to do so.

Ethiopia: I would like to go next.

Australia: Excellent. Begin.

Ethiopia: While it is true that Christianity and Islam took hold on my continent over a thousand years ago, there are religions that are much, much older.

Yoruba, a Nigerian religion, has survived the onslaught of these Euro-Asian interlopers and is still quietly practiced throughout the world, especially in Benin, Togo, the United States of America, the United Kingdom, Cuba, Brazil, and Trinidad and Tobago, where people of color have not forgotten their roots.

Even other offshoot derivative religions like **Santeria** have embraced its influence.

The Celestial Pure **Obatala, King of the White Cloth,**

is rumored to be the son of **Olorun**, one of the three manifestations of the Supreme God, along with **Olodumare**, the Creator, and **Olofi**. Obatala was the founder of the first Yoruba city, Ife.

Obatala, also known as **Orisha-Nla** or **Olufon**, is the eldest of all **Orisha** (deities). He entered into a legendary battle with a rival Celestial, **Oduduwa**, who, after defeating Obatala, was permitted to rule over the land with His sons, as long as They respected the Covenant and did not attempt to re-enslave the people.

A **Babalawo** is a priest, and thus a consultant on geomantic divination. He provides insight and passes on the guidance he receives from the **ikin**, or **Divination Chain** given to man by **Orunmila**, the spirit of wisdom. Others use stones, bones, cowrie shells, and coins that land in a positive or negative sequence.

It was believed, at one time, that the Gods themselves influenced the falling of the stones, but this has never been true. Fate, or chance, has always been the arbiter of the toss.

Divination is mankind's way of seeking answers to life's endless questions; Man's plea for guidance from the spirit world. Man's attempt to alter his fate by changing his path.

Does it work? Does prayer work? Does common sense work? You tell me.

What can I say about **Voodoo**, or **Vodun** as it is called in West Africa. Vodun began with the worship of the Celestial Pure **Nana Buluku**, who gave birth to the twins **Mawa** and **Lisa** or **Mawa-Lisa**, the Creator Goddess.

Suffice it to say that much was lost and much was added by the displaced African slaves and their descendants over the centuries who developed the superstitiously based Voodoo.

New Orleans' Voodoo Queen, **Marie Laveau**, a Sub-pure, rose to prominence by blending her Catholic faith with her voodoo practice. She was known to perform exorcisms as well as offering sacrifices to the spirits.

I am trying to find a non-abrasive way to approach this religion. There are two points I would like to make.

Firstly, it is impossible to negatively impact someone else's spirit without also damaging your own. Every curse and hex you evoke, or have evoked on your behalf, becomes part of who you are, in the same way that it only takes one murder for you to forever see yourself as a murderer. You cannot fool you.

I understand the need to seek some semblance of control over one's fate as it is being negatively influenced by another's will, but one must take care as to what length one is willing to go for retribution.

Secondly, it is difficult to tell whether it is the disadvantaged who seek out voodoo solutions, or whether it is the practice of voodoo itself which leads to one being disadvantaged. Does the tail ultimately end up wagging the dog?

Superstition dictates behavior and thus becomes a pathway to unhealthy obsession. Voodoo's obsession with spiritual possession and the manipulation of others opens the doors to the spiritual and mental corruption of the practitioner. Therefore, one should tread very carefully. Or better yet, choose a different path that does not require a **gris-gris** or **Voodoo Dolls**.

Look around you and see that the majority of those who do not practice Voodoo also do not suffer the same level of spiritual and financial degradation as those who do.

Confusion leads to desperation. Order stems from information. How we process that information is oftentimes shaped by our beliefs and our superstitions. But trust me, some answers are not to be found on the Internet or within a given religion, but only through deep inner reflection.

Australia: Very enlightening. Who's next?

Britain: I know you have all been anxiously waiting to hear from the resident Witch, so I will keep you in suspense no longer.

You're all gonna die. The end. Thank you very much.

Just kidding…or not.

Wicca is the proper name for modern **Pagan Witchcraft** today. It is considered a bonafide religion, much to the surprise and dismay of many Christians, who would rather deem it **Devil worship**, which it most certainly is not.

Wicca is divided into various "traditions" and has no central authority figure to define it.

Wicca is traditionally a duotheistic religion that pays homage to both a
Triple Goddess,

associated with the Moon and stars and fate, and a **Horned God**.

Who said **Satan**? I *dare* you to say it again!
Anyway, it's **Cernunnos**, or **Pan**,

who some claim was just one example of a successful Celestial Pure experiment in **gene splicing**, like the **Minotaur**, **Horus** and a few other well-known hybrids.

The practice of gene splicing was forbidden on Earth, however; therefore, it is difficult to find any confirmation concerning these matters, and many have chosen to believe that they are purely the stuff of Myth anyway. Yeah, right.

Okay, let's cut the crap. Cernunnos was a Celestial Pure who some believe was a son of Zeus, and who apparently was tasked with looking after Earth animals, whom He liked more than people. He enjoyed parading around in a hat with stag horns on it. No, he didn't really have goat horns or hooves. Some clown of a playwright or artist added them for dramatic effect, and the image stuck.

There are still the ruins of temples built in his honor in caves and on the Neda River gorge in the Peloponnese region of Greece and at Apollonopolis Magna in Egypt.

Listen, we traditional Witches call Wicca "weak and wack," because it's full of a bunch of "Witch wannabes." They've been seeking acceptance and legitimacy since their inception. Frankly, Traditional Witches don't much care what the "Muggles" think.

Irish Traditional Witches, like myself, do not belong to a religion. Our roots are ancient and our ways are proven.

Yes, we still cast spells, make poultices, heal the sick, tell fortunes and commune with spirits, just as we always have; but as you can see, we're not all ugly with huge nose warts, and we don't ride around on broomsticks, even though some of us could if we wanted to.

We find most movies about witches hilarious.

Remember when I told you that the Pure Colony, Hy-Brasil, disappeared during the Great Departure? Well, the resident Pures who preferred to stay on Earth were relocated to the British Isles.

If you think about it for a moment, it's easy to understand how They brought Their advanced knowledge of pharmacology with Them. That, coupled with the ability to read minds and precognitive insight, intrigued some and frightened others. All went fairly well until Christianity reared its ugly little head and they began persecuting Us.

Many **Shaman** throughout the ancient world were also Earth Pures, along with **Oracles, Magi, Seers, Sorcerers, Witch Doctors, Wizards, Warlocks** (who are actually called Male Witches), and **Witches.**

There is no "**Black Magic**" or "**White Magic,**" just **Magic,** which can be used for good or for evil; kind of like a gun. The same applies to **Voodoo, Hoodoo** and **Juju.**

Most so-called "Witches" today are Sub-pures or Taints. Their ability to effectively tell the future or to speak with spirits is greatly diminished compared to that of We Pure Witches, who are now *forbidden* to publicly practice Our Craft, or as most call it, "Witchcraft". We learned the hard way where that leads. Is anyone here in the mood to be burned at the stake or drowned?

Non-pures will try just about anything to attempt to control their destinies, or at least try to convince themselves that they can somehow manipulate the unseen forces that be, or bend the world around them to their wills through prayer or superstitiously based rituals.

And why not? They're supposed to be able to do those things, and intuitively they still know it. But for Us, it's kind of like watching an infant try to walk. There's a lot of falling, failing and fizzling.

Australia: Very nice, Ms. Britain. Who's next?

Russia: As most of you know, Russia took a pretty hard stance against religion many years ago. And although we have long since relaxed our basic tenets, for some reason we are still believed to primarily be **Atheists.**

One of the problems with **Atheism** is the problem of certainty. If I am certain that there is no God, then how am I any better than you are, if you are certain that there is one? Do I possess some absolute knowledge that you do not? Or am I just taking the stance that since you cannot prove to me that God exists, then He doesn't?

Well, I cannot prove to you that I truly love my wife and children, or that love itself truly exists at all, but that doesn't mean that I don't feel something deep down inside me that is real and undeniable, even if it is not irrefutably verifiable.

After all, you can fake love just like you can fake faith.

Most Atheists are actually **Agnostics** in denial. We're aware that we don't *really* know the truth, but pride and arrogance prohibit us from openly admitting it.

Most Pures consider Themselves to be either Agnostics or Atheists because Our people have been down this road for eons. Not only that, but because We are well aware of the lies and manipulations of Our Celestial ancestors, We cannot pretend as if any of Earth's religions are true.

Don't get me wrong. I do not despise others for wanting to believe in a fairy tale. I just don't understand how they can walk around trying to get others to believe in it with them. Or how they can read the so-called Holy text in front of them and not see it as contradictory nonsense.

Look, don't hate me for being so skeptical, and I won't hate you for being so naïve. After all, we're only Human, which very well may be a synonym for "innately flawed".

Our ancestors have traversed the universe, and I promise you that We have found no true gods there; except for the ones found in people's imaginations.

Maybe I have said too much, but Pure brains just don't process information that way. Things have to make logical sense for Us to believe them…and no earth-made religion does.

Australia:	Sobering and to the point. Thank you, Mr. Russia. Mr. Washington?
Washington:	What a Scrooge! *"There is no Santa Claus, there is no Easter Bunny, there is no God!"* Let them have their little fantasies as long as they're not hurting anyone.

Oh yeah, they're killing each other by the thousands over it, aren't they?

Well, the ancient tribes of North America had good reason to believe in the "**Star Beings**". After all, they met with Them, mated with Them and learned from Them.

They still profess to occasionally meeting with Them today.

Native Americans do not share one religion, but they do share many fundamental beliefs that overlap their varied traditions.

One of these fundamental truths is that they came from the stars. They have not forgotten, unlike most of the people of this world, who they are. Some tribes point out the Pleiades star system as their place of origin.

The **Star Nations** are being told by the **Star Visitors**, of the approaching end of the **Fourth World** and the emergence of the Fifth World, which should lead to a thousand years of peace. They have been told that "*We are coming.*"

The history of such visitations can be traced back even before the visit of the
White Buffalo Calf Woman

of the Lakota (**Sioux**), who gave them a **Chanunpa,** or sacred ceremonial **Calf Pipe.**

Most tribes believe that through the use of the **Sweat Lodge** and the **Sacred** or **Ceremonial Pipe** (most white men refer to it as a "**Peace pipe**"), one's mind is opened to pray to and communicate with the Creator and/or the Star People above.

Native Americans, by and large, do not separate the natural from the supernatural. Their own brand of **Panantheism** suggests that the world is not just infused with God/the Divine and consciousness, like **Pantheism** (which holds that the Divine is synonymous with the universe), but that Nature and the universe are also contained *within* God or the Divine, Who/Which extends beyond it.

The concept of **Wakan Tanka**, the Sioux way of life, which is translated as "**The Great Spirit**" or "**The Great Mystery**," allows for the existence of a confluence of spirits.

The **Iroquois** and **Algonquians** believe the benevolent Great Spirit has an evil brother, **Hanegoategeh.**

The **Apache**, due to their oftentimes harsh living conditions, had little time for religious ritual, so they concentrated instead on supernatural cultural figures. They established their own relationships with the supernatural to manipulate Their powers, like the **Apache Mountain Spirit Dance** and the **Rain Dance**, which is also performed by the **Zuni, Osage**, and **Quapaw** tribes, among many others.

Shamanism linked the Apache people, and others, to the healing power of the supernatural world.

A **Vision Quest** is a rite of passage performed by a twelve- to fifteen-year-old boy or girl who spends four days and nights in solitude, oftentimes fasting. They are secluded in Nature in order to gain spiritual guidance, insight and a deeper understanding of their purpose in life.

If prepared well enough, a **Weyekin** or **Wyakin**—a helping spirit, usually in the form of an animal, like a deer, buffalo, fox, bear or bird—will approach the questor in a vision and be adopted, lending their animal attributes to them in times of need.

No other Non-pures on Earth are more in tune with who they are and should be than the Native American Indian, but their dogmatic approach to remaining true to themselves has rendered them the victims of a fate imposed upon them by others.

And yet they wait patiently, believing the day is coming when their unvarnished relationship with Nature and the way things are supposed to be, will not only be exonerated but appreciated, and that their wise counsel will ultimately be enthusiastically sought after.

Australia: Well, that was unexpected and praiseworthy. Thank you for your candor.

Egypt: Would you mind if I go next?

Australia: No, go right ahead.

Egypt: Who needs religion when you actually live with your very own flesh-and-bone Gods?

Well, apparently we did. Praise and reverence were both expected and demanded by the Celestial Pures who established the great kingdoms in Egypt.

Amun-Ra, a Celestial Pure Overseer, was betrayed by **Isis**, who quickly installed as King, Her brother **Osiris**, who was married to Their sister **Nephthys**, but to whom She, Isis, was a consort anyway, and bore Their child Horus, who became the King of Egypt after He overthrew **Set** (Seth) after Set had killed His father/uncle Osiris.

Set   Ramesses II   Horus

And thus soap operas were born! Umm humm, I'm just sayin', girl.

Anyway, some King or Queen set about enslaving all of the Non-pures from hundreds of miles around to erect the pyramids, as well as others to help sustain those workers by providing them with housing, food and clothing.

Egyptian "Gods" and rulers apparently liked to walk around wearing elaborate headpieces to distinguish Themselves from one another, and to evoke awe and reverence from those who served Them. I guess animal heads provided a little additional panache to the artwork.

Tell me something. Why do Non-pures today insist on trying to take ancient people so literally, when they know full well that those people were abjectly incapable of understanding what was actually going on, most, if not all of the time? Excuse me, did I say *ancient* people?

Upon death, whether staged or true, the ancient Celestial and Earth Pures (particularly those of status) were guaranteed to have Their remains lifted up and returned to Their planet of origin for a proper traditional burial.

To facilitate this, the practice of **mummification** was implemented along with the construction of the pyramids; some of which were meant to be temporary holding places for the "royal remains" until a local mothership was scheduled to return home, at which time those deemed worthy were exhumed.

Many believe that this is where the concept of one's soul going up to Heaven began, since this removal process was practiced all over the Earth, on behalf of the early Celestial and Earth Pures.

Unfortunately, the practice was discontinued when it was found that the customary method of disposing of what were now considered "Earthly remains" threatened to permanently contaminate the home planet's ecosystem.

After the "Great Leaving," it was noticed that the Kings, or Pharaohs, no longer seemed to have direct access to the Higher Gods. Most of them were Sub-pures, or Taints by then, and were unfortunately left behind with the Non-pures.

It became a common practice to appeal to the new "Gods" for help or favors through individual and collective prayer.

Attempting to compel Them to act through magic, also grew as a viable option.

Oh yeah, the Earth Pure **Akhenaten, or Amenhotep IV,** as He was known, sought to install the Celestial Pure "sun god" **Aten** as the monotheistic God of the Egyptian people. Coincidentally, access to Aten was restricted, except through Akhenaten Himself, as the sole intermediary. This lasted for only twenty or so years before His successors, later led by Tutankhamun (previously known as Tutankhaten), returned to the worship of Amun, and the older more accepted religious practices. Subsequently, Akhenaten's name and image were all but completely expunged from most temple sites and records.

The **Hyksos,**

who were led by Earth Pures, were brought to Egypt by the Celestial Overseer Baal (aka Seth), who sought to rekindle Egyptian greatness after the decline brought about by the Great Leaving. They brought with them the chariot, new musical instruments, new breeds of animals, new crops and the composite bow.

By decree, there are no more known Pure political or religious leaders on the planet Earth today. But, many of Us are still stealthily running things from behind the scenes.

All I will say about Islam, due to the insane animosity its adherents have towards anyone who questions its tenets, is that the more egregiously sensitive one is about a subject or belief, the more one has to hide, or is ashamed of, their lack of understanding of it.

I would implore all Muslims not to allow radical Islamists to continue to subvert control over their religion through the oppressive shackles of narrowly redefined faith and devotion.

The jihadists among them have also taken to violently condemning any remaining tolerance of non-Muslims and of all other contrary belief systems.

Islam's growing disdain towards all others has permanently damaged its self-proclaimed reputation as a now highly dubious "religion of peace."

For hundreds of years Muslims have been at war with the Jews, Hindus, Buddhists and Christians, and now they're at war with other Muslims.

I shudder to think what will happen if the world wakes up and inevitably unites against those who would seek to eradicate or enslave all of mankind in the name of **Allah**.

Tolerance, like a prayer rug, wears thin on both sides.

This cannot end well.

Australia: That was quite thought provoking.

Rome?

Rome: We came, we saw, and we conquered!

Few know that it was Earth Pures who convinced "Yahweh" (Avinu) to use his son Jesus to hand over Judaism, in the guise of Christianity, to the gentiles, and ultimately free His people from Roman dominance. What a coup!

That foot on the neck thing works really well!

The Jews *hated* the fact that we appropriated their religion, because it was the only thing in the world they could hold over the Romans after the way we had treated them. So, they begged the local emperor to slaughter all the turncoat, traitorous new Christian converts. He didn't truly care one way or the other, because they were seen as zealots and not as Roman citizens. Crucify them, feed them to the lions, why should any true Roman care?

Eventually, however, with a tactical act of sheer brilliance, **Emperor Constantine** saw to it that Roman Catholicism was born; and it is still thriving to this day!

Jews are still sitting around in denial that "Yahweh" actually sanctioned Christianity; so much so that they're still, to this day, wandering around waiting for Immanuel to show up. They simply refuse to believe that He already has. C'mon, guys, it was your prophecy after all!

Bloodthirsty Romans in Heaven—who'd a thunk it?

Rome stole a religion and they've been stealing ever since.   Pass the collection plate, please. We'll make sure God gets His fair share.

Who's a cynic? I'm a realist. After all, We *know* who God was.

And you forget that I live at the Vatican. Talk about a bunch of insincere posers!

They know darn well that the Councils of Nicaea and Constantinople got together and cooked the books! They decided to ignore what Jesus said about his "Father" calling the shots, and instead decided to make the two of Them the same person? A Trinity, really?

Don't get me wrong, Jesus was a great guy… arguably one of the greatest of all time, but We all know who His mommy was, so how do you start equating Him with God? So, He's his own father?

(Well, there is that cloning thing.)

And then they sat around editing the Bible itself. They changed names, they deleted whole books, they redacted and subtracted at will. Who does that and then still has the unmitigated gall to insist that it's the Holy Word of God Himself?

Every one of them knows that God didn't write or dictate a single word of the "Holy Bible." If He had, they wouldn't have *dared* change any part of it; and every Bishop, Cardinal, and the very Pope himself, knows it.

The contradictions are so prevalent as to be laughable. First He made the animals and then Adam. No, first He made Adam, who was lonely, so He made the animals. Okaaaaay.

How could anyone be mad at me for simply pointing out the truth? I'm not lying and they all know it. Did I really burst anyone's sacred bubble?

Now, is the Bible worth keeping around? Hell, yes! It's a wonderful book and I wish everyone, including You Pures, would follow its advice.

"Yahweh" had a great idea. Jesus was a great man. The Bible is a wonderful book of anecdotal moral lessons, just like the Torah and the Koran.

Why are you all looking at me like that? What more do you want from me?

Australia: Nothing. Sit down. One day you're going to figure out that it's all in the delivery.

Would you like to go next, Israel?

Israel: After that?…Hell yeah!

Oy vey! Sometimes a divine blessing feels a little like a curse.

At the risk of being severely chastised, I am going to divulge a little historical information that would probably prove daunting to some outside of this room.

As We all know, it was a succession of Celestial Pures who set about converting the pagan religions of a given region into a religion that honored and prayed to Them as their local Creator God or Divine Benefactor.

In a nutshell, The Celestial Pure, **El**, later called **Elohim** (plural) by the Hebrews, or **Enlil** by the Sumerians, was the God of **Noah** and the Canaanites. He destroyed countless lives by requisitioning his brother **Enki** to create a **regional flood**, as *other* Celestials had previously done in other regions.

A *different* Celestial Pure, we'll call **Yahweh,** was the God of **Abraham,** the Earth Pure.

Yahweh was not a very forgiving ruler either, and was known to be both cruel and vindictive. He insisted on unflinching loyalty and fealty. Yahweh, however, was no longer around by the time the Celestial Pure known as **Allah,** via his messenger **Muhammad,** founded **Islam.**

Jehovah was still another Celestial Pure who sought to leave His own personal stamp on this planet via deception and coerced devotion.

For some reason the Hebrews resisted Yahweh's offer to make them **The Chosen People** if they would but worship only Him. Not only were they told that they would be His "**Treasured People**" but that the **Messiah,** or redeemer of the world, would come from them.

Still, their loyalty waned both before and after they entered into the **Covenant** He made with them, and subsequently, Yahweh punished the Hebrews with drought, famine, persecution, and eventually, enslavement.

You would think that they would have fallen in line after that, but good old **Polytheism** kept beckoning them back.

Still another Celestial Pure, **Adonai**, the God of **Moses**, freed the Hebrews from Egypt and gave them His **Ten Commandments.**

But this was apparently still not enough to garner devoutness. Seeing that they were, again, returning to their pagan heritage, even after watching Him part the sea on their behalf, Adonai spitefully stranded them in the desert for 40 years to give them sufficient time to reconsider His offer to lead them to **The Promised Land, Israel.**

And yes, you guessed it, it was the Celestial Pure **Avinu** who actually later fathered **Imman,** or **Jesus** as most call him.

It should be obvious that none of these were their *real* names, but instead, names that were given to them by the Hebrews, who later insisted that they were all the same God, Yahweh. But *We* know better, don't We?

It should be equally obvious that a single "God" did not keep changing His mind. It was different "Gods" with different approaches to inspiring undivided allegiance, and not one schizophrenic individual who kept the Jews in a permanent state of uncertainty and angst.

Unfortunately, once the Jews finally got the message and swore a permanent allegiance to their Lord, all the other surrounding nations began to resent them more than ever for considering themselves "chosen" over all others. Heaven was only within the grasp of the select Jewish few, while all others were, by birthright, unfairly locked out.

Avinu and Jesus recognized that this would always be a source of animus toward the Jews, and so allowed everyone else in through a back door of Their own devising. Through the acceptance of Avinu's possibly cloned son, "Jesus", as the **Messiah**, any former heathenistic reprobate could now gain access to the formerly inaccessible, although never verifiable, Hebrew Heaven.

The Jews rightfully felt betrayed by "God" because they had already paid so dearly for keeping His Word and adhering to the demands of the Old Covenants of the **Torah**. They now justifiably felt that they were being religiously depreciated by the imposition of Jesus' **New Covenant** with the **Gentiles**. Oy, the chutzpah!

What happened to the "chosen people" part of the Abrahamic and Mosaic Covenants? And so they rejected the perceived interloper Jesus, which ticked off His Celestial Father, and once again set themselves against the growing multitude of adherents to the new **Christian** faith.

In the centuries to come, their refusal to acknowledge Jesus as the true son of God and the prophesied Messiah got the Jewish people expelled from numerous locations outside of Israel.

In 1215, the Catholic Church had Jews segregated into areas called **ghettos**. In 1290, they were expelled from England.

Shortly thereafter, the Jews were expelled from France.

In 1492, the Jews were expelled from Spain.

In 1497, the Jews were expelled from Portugal.

In the 1700s, the Russians restricted them to living in areas called **The Pale of Settlement**, which later included parts of Poland.

Eventually, in the mid-19th century, the **Zionist** movement began in an effort to create a Jewish state.

An estimated 6 million Jewish people were murdered during the **Holocaust**, and neither Celestial nor Earth Pures were permitted to do anything about it. That is until 1948, when behind the cover of worldwide outrage and guilt-ridden politics, Earth Pures and others advocated for the establishment of the State of Israel.

Pures have long memories, and the part Celestials played in singling out the Hebrews to further their hidden personal agendas is now considered sordid and borderline reprehensible. Most Celestials have taken an oath to never engage in such practices again.

B'nai B'rith was founded with the help of at least one Earth Pure. It is dedicated to combating **Antisemitism** and bigotry. And the fight continues.

Jews for Jesus consists of members who consider themselves to be Jews, either by parentage, as a birthright, or as defined by Jewish law. They focus on the conversion of Jews to Christianity.

Jewish religious denominations and other Jewish groups reject their identification as a Jewish organization, and their conservative evangelical stance invites mixed reactions from Christian organizations. In other words, they're now getting it from both sides. Even Jews can find a way to ostracize other Jews for not conforming. And the beat goes on.

Kabbalah seeks to define the nature of the Universe and of the Human Being. Maybe I can help lend some insight into part of that.

Embrace the fact that reality is grounded in reality, whereas mysticism is grounded in speculation, misinterpretation and at times desperation.

However, any sincerely legitimate attempt to better understand the universe and one's place in it is to be applauded, so long as no artificial means of mental stimulation via drugs or deprivation are employed, since they oftentimes lead to erroneous experiences that can best be described as hallucinations and not truth.

Seeking the truth is and should be a lifelong quest, but *how* one proceeds along the path to further enlightenment is just as informative as anything one might discover along the way.

Meditation, a form of which many Earth Pures practice to some lesser extent, when coupled with honesty and truthfulness, is admirable, but when coupled with contrivance and artificiality, it only contributes to confusion, and not truth or knowledge. If the precepts are flawed, the road will only lead to questionable conjecture at best.

For example, **Ezekiel**

indeed saw something; but it was not "God" or a "Chariot."

If asked how an iPad works, for lack of a better explanation, he may have told you that tiny little people live inside it. He would have most certainly lacked the prerequisite vocabulary and understanding to adequately describe what he had actually witnessed.

The Jewish Nation needs protection, both from its enemies and from its divisive dogmatism.

Australia: I didn't see that coming. Would you like to go next, Japan?

Japan: Of course.

                    Few people realize that over 70% of the Japanese populace consider themselves to be **non-religious**. They're not really Atheists; they're just non-affiliated.

Shinto,  meaning "**The Way of the Gods,**" is the indigenous religion of Japan, and was primarily based on nature worship. Their gods or spirits, which imbued everything from rocks to trees and streams, are called **Kami,** who insist on physical and spiritual cleanliness.

Legend has it that the Celestial Pures **Izanagi** and **Izanami**

created Japan from *droplets* of water that dripped down from Izanagi's *spear*.

How they imagined this explanation from the fact that their regional Celestial Pure Overseer and his "wife" *dropped* them off on the islands from their *spacecraft* to protect them from being re-enslaved on mainland China, I'll never understand. They later gave birth to a deity daughter, **Amaterasu**.

Shinto developed into three separate forms, which included **Shrine Shinto**, **Folk Shinto**, which was practiced by the peasants, and **Imperial Household Shinto**, which was practiced by the imperial house of Japan.

Shinto began to decline when Buddhism came to Japan, but it was soon found that both were being practiced together. During the **Meiji Restoration** they were united once again, with Shinto becoming the official religion called **State Shinto**, which merged Shrine, Folk and Imperial Household Shinto into one.

State Shinto also became the official religion of Korea and Taiwan, after Japan took them over.

During World War II the Japanese government insisted that the Emperor should be considered Divine, but when the United States occupied Japan in 1945, State Shinto was abolished and the three forms of Shinto separated once again.

Is anybody bored yet?

Christianity, Islam, Hinduism, Judaism, Taoism, Jainism,

Baha'i,  and **Ryukyuan** also have a small presence in Japan. Still wonder why most Japanese people say they're non-affiliated?

The Zen in **Zen Buddhism**

reflects the serene attitude with which the practitioner should pursue spiritual enlightenment. Meditating for hours while using **koans,** or nonsensical riddles, like "What is the sound of one hand clapping?", is said to free the mind of its concerns about daily life.

Confucianism 水 , Chinese astrology and feng shui (earth study) have also crept into the complex Japanese spiritual life.

Australia: Thank you, Japan. India, I believe you are the last to share.

India: That is what the best is usually reserved for, is it not?

               India is the birthplace of four of the world's major religions, namely

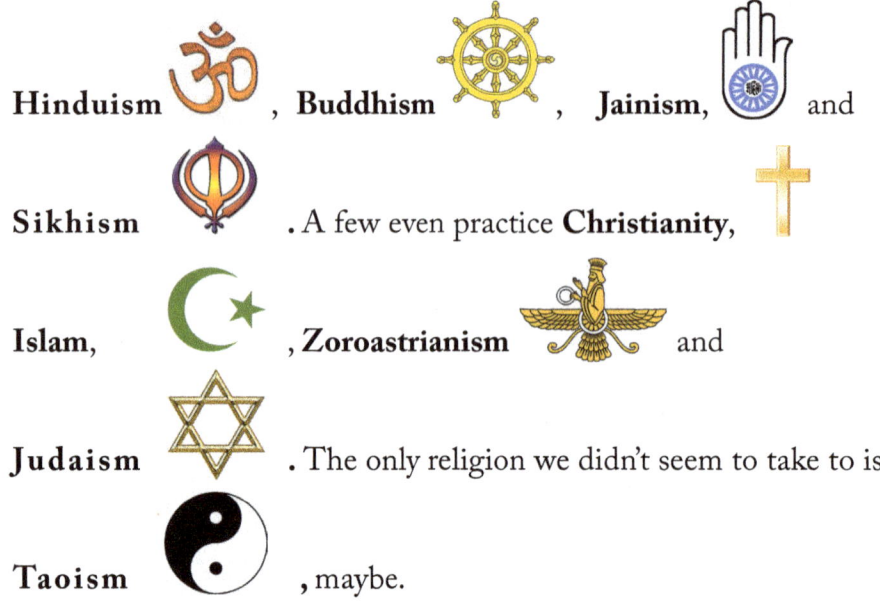

Hinduism , Buddhism , Jainism, and

Sikhism . A few even practice **Christianity**,

Islam, , **Zoroastrianism** and

Judaism . The only religion we didn't seem to take to is

Taoism , maybe.

That is why religious tolerance is enforced by the law. Unlike Japan, over 90% of Indians claim affiliation with some religion.

Yoga , a Hindu practice, is a form of meditation, or torture, depending on who you ask.

Karma is the concept that most aligns itself with "Celestial and Earth Pure Spirituality."

Although some, like Hindu followers, believe that God is involved in karma, most Buddhists believe that it is the **natural laws of cause and effect** that govern karma. Karma is not punishment or retribution but simply an extended expression or consequence of one's actions. Therefore, it is cause and effect, action and reaction, that governs one's life, although it is not to be seen as a simple one-to-one association of reward or punishment.

Karma is not **fate**, because free-willed humans create their own destiny, and one's actions today may indeed be mitigated by one's actions tomorrow.

The **Vedas** say, "If one sows goodness, one will reap goodness; if one sows evil, one will reap evil." The conquest of karma lies in intelligent action and dispassionate response.

Yes, there are some who call themselves **Hindu Atheists**, but please don't hurt your brains thinking about it too much.

Reincarnation (Dazu Wheel)

is the religious or philosophical belief that the spirit or soul will come back in the body of a human, an animal, or as a spirit, depending upon the moral quality of one's previous life's actions.

Where they get this crazy stuff from, I don't know. For years I've been looking for somebody I knew in another life, and I've never recognized a single soul. Besides, what good is being reborn to get things right if I don't even remember who I was or what I did wrong before that kept me here on Earth?

I should have ascended by now! I should have attained Nirvana! Instead I'm stuck here with you numbskulls. I'm damned near perfect, so how am I supposed to correct for mistakes I don't even remember making?

Beam me up, Scotty!

I'm sorry. Where was I?

Oh, yes. This is what happens when a few Celestials start competing for the minds of the poor unsuspecting masses below. Most of these religions are incongruent with one another, and yet everyone is running around trying to believe them all at the same time, or at the very least, trying to pick out the colorful lie they like the most.

Why can't Mutes see that Someone just made this stuff up? You ascend to Nirvana, you go to Heaven, you come back in another body, you don't come back or go anywhere at all. There is a God, there is no God, there are lots of gods, Nature is a god, that rock is a god, my shapely ass is a god. I frankly can't take it anymore!

Shrines, temples, and early mosques and churches were built as places to communicate with the **Celestials** above, if They happened to be listening. Can't they tell that there's nobody paying them any attention anymore? The Celestials posing as Gods all got recalled for Their reprehensible manipulative behavior, during the Great Leaving!

The lights are out and nobody's home!

Heaven help me, a wood nymph just told me that I just screwed up my karma again. Next time I'll probably come back as a weasel!

Australia: It'll be okay. Just take a deep breath. Were you finished?

India: Apparently I'll never be finished. I'm doomed to go to Hell as a skunk!

Australia.   Hummm. Well then, I guess it's best if I take the floor.

               First I have a few observations to make.

Freemasonry, a pseudo religion, began as an admiration society for **Euclid** the Pure, who is regarded as the father of geometry.

Masonic Lodges were started by male Earth Pures who collectively decided to meet at regular intervals to discuss local affairs and global concerns. **Anglo Saxon Freemasonry**, as it took root in England, required their select membership to be White, male, and Christian, and forbade the discussion of politics.

Continental Freemasonry later evolved as a response to the exclusivity of Anglo-Saxon Freemasonry. Unlike its cousin, it permits, depending upon the region, the membership of other ethnic groups, women, freedom of religion and the discussion of politics.

Both divisions have lost sight of the origins of Free Masonry, which transitioned away from its initial intent when the Taint and Mute sons of Pures began to fill the lodges and eventually pushed the Pures out as they embraced religion as one of their focal points.

The **Roman Catholics** and others have since responded by excommunicating members of the allegedly "Occult" Free Masons from the Church itself.

Free Masons were instrumental in the formulation of the United States of America. But an interesting aside to the entire book of speculation, as to just how deeply involved they were, is to be found on the back of American currency itself.

The Pyramid was actually put there by Free Masons to remind everyone that it was engineered by Celestial Pures, Who were the original   architects of the new world.   The All-Seeing Eye is there to connote the omnipotence of the Celestials as They are still observing Earthkind today from Their spacecraft above.

The nonsensical pseudo-religious **Freemasonry Rituals** and contrived mysticism that still pervade the Lodges today (which are, unfortunately, still steeped in secrecy) only serve to cling to a time and place where logic and reason were paramount, but have long since given way to trite illegitimacy.

Despite claims made by the **Mormon Church** , there are no official or unofficial records to be found that verify whether or not **Joseph Smith** ever met with a Celestial Pure or "angel" named **Maroni** in New York; or that he ever received the now conveniently missing golden **"Plates of Nephi"** from Him.

Their practices of **polygamy** and **communal living** have been looked down upon with great suspicion and oftentimes condemnation by the Christian church.

As far as Celestial Pures are concerned, the entire story is fictitious due to the fact that Jesus himself never sat foot on the North American continent after He was "resurrected."

Therefore, **Mormonism** and the **Church of Jesus Christ of Latter-day Saints** are considered purely man-made concoctions and not the product of Celestial manipulation.

Scientology , likewise, is solely man's attempt to manipulate and control man. It is undeniable   that its founder, **L. Ron Hubbard**, had a brilliant mind. Although his methods and intentions are questionable, it is irrefutable that the man sought to free mankind from its obsession with the material, and encourage them to seek spiritual growth.

Many Pures believe that Mr. Hubbard had been approached and informed by a rogue Pure as to mankind's dilemma as it pertains to religion.

Somehow, somewhere Mr. Hubbard took this knowledge and embellished greatly upon it. He allowed the science fiction novel writer inside of himself to run wild with basic concepts and infuse those concepts with purely speculative conjecture.

In other words, he made up most of his theoretical teachings and sold them as scientific or religious fact. Much of what he proffers is either erroneous, ridiculous, an outright lie or intrinsically non-verifiable.

The "Church," in his absence, has seen fit to alienate all of those who would question his teachings and speak out against the Church's alleged practices of brainwashing and coercion, with threats of **disconnection**, exile, excommunication and lawsuits.

Secrecy and the mystical **OT levels** of **thetan** development, which supposedly lead one toward a better understanding of one's immortality, have lent an air of **Cultism** to the questionable religion, in which so much is dubious and so little is quantifiable.

As We are all aware, the **spirit/soul**, like thoughts, is in fact, a material or physical thing. Hubbard himself said it has weight. As such, no claims of immortality can be assured, since all matter devolves, degrades or changes with time. He was told this, and yet he chose to placate his disciples with promises of immortality that he knew could never be assured, and were most likely fallacious at best. Bequeathing the Church of Scientology much, if not all, of your worldly possessions, is also a practice common to cults.

L. Ron Hubbard got many things right, but his teachings are significantly diminished by the things that he and/or the Church got wrong. And all who attempt to embrace Scientology's teachings become increasingly aware of its shortcomings, or ultimately abandon all common sense to his faith-based dogma.

The Baha'i Faith seeks to find the commonality between most major religions and to claim that they are all united by their allegiance to the one same God they all worship.

This could not be further from the truth. It's merely wishful thinking at its best. They should be commended for their efforts to find or establish unity, but their presuppositions are fatally flawed and their "One God" remains, now and forever, nonexistent. The ancient "Gods" that inspired the various Earth religions were never one and the same, and insisting that they were will, nonetheless, never make it true.

Their ultimate goal of religiously unifying humanity is perhaps the most praiseworthy of all of the disparate religions, but insight and enlightenment will eventually bring about the demise of all manufactured faith-based belief systems, no matter how well-intentioned they may be.

A personal pet peeve of mine is the illogical and yet widely adhered-to belief that "When it's your time to go, it's your time to go.". That is one of the most spurious, nonsensical, ill-conceived, ignorant utterances I've ever come across.

It entails the belief that if a jumbo jet crashes into a skyscraper, each of the passengers aboard, as well as each of the soon-to-be extinguished lives of those sitting innocently at their work stations, were led there by their predetermined and inescapable fates, to die at that precise moment in time.

Led there by what malicious homicidal Supreme Being?

You've got to be kidding me!

Some sick God is handing out boarding passes, entry cards and subway tokens? And the questionably lucky few who happen to have survived the catastrophe, but are permanently psychically scarred and/or physically impaired, have supposedly received some sort of Divine pardon? They're the fortunate ones, because God or Fate determined that it just wasn't quite "their time to go"? The same God or Fate decided to make some firefighters and policemen surviving heroes, and yet condemned others to be mourned victims?

How inhumane would you have to be to compile that bloody list? How stoically naïve do you have to be to believe that there is that degree of meticulously premeditated dire intention behind that degree of incalculable uncertainty and chaotically circumstantial unpredictability?

Let's face it, life is sometimes unjustifiably unfair. Most alleged "fate" is dependent upon hindsight being 20/20. Not all consequences are preordained or predetermined. Sometimes luck and chance are momentarily on our side and, at other times, regrettably not. Sometimes there is no rational reason behind, or teachable lesson to be learned from unforeseen tragedy.

In other words, fortune, like religion, can be a duplicitous and unreliable bitch.

Multitudes of desperate prayers inside those buildings were completely ignored.

Benevolent, faith-filled hearts were callously crushed.

Undeserving, angelic voices were forever silenced.

I lost a very dear friend on 9/11. And I dare anyone to suggest that it was simply because "it was her time to go."

Religion killed her...

(Complete silence for fifteen seconds)

Please forgive my momentary lapse into melancholy. Even I am only human.

So, where do we go from here?

We have learned that no two religions completely agree on the *source* or *method* of creation, or on mankind's true inception and any definitively divine intent behind it. They can't agree on where, if anywhere, the spirit/soul goes upon true death, or on any of the other nagging questions concerning the fundamentals of human spirituality.

By definition this would insist that all religions but one must, by necessity, be untrue or, at the very least, irreparably flawed.

Of course, everyone chooses to believe that *their* religion is based on the "real" truth, while all the others are just flailing about spouting their superstitiously based rhetoric.

And lest some of You have forgotten, Our ancient Pure ancestors once naively believed in an highly speculative, nonverifiable **Creation Deity** They called "The Keeper of the Globe."

That said, does anyone have any serious suggestions as to what can or should be done about this?

Russia: Abolish all religion!

Washington: Let's just sit back and wait for them to completely annihilate each other.

Britain: Why don't we just tell them the truth?

India: Why don't we just walk away and leave them alone?

Israel: Turn them all into Jews!

Rome: Allow us to beat them into submission.

Japan: Promote **Hara-kiri**?

Australia: I said *serious* suggestions.

China: He *was* being serious.

Ethiopia: Force them to agree on one religion.

Peru: Find a way to make them pay to pray.

Egypt: Let Us retrain them in the "Pure Way" of spiritual enlightenment.

Australia: Well, I guess this is as good a time as any to explain the *Celestial Religion Agenda*.

At the beginning of this Summit, I informed You all that We were given four scenarios. The second scenario was Subjugation. After a considerable amount of discussion and contemplation, my Father has informed me that Our Celestial brothers have devised a possible avenue of facilitating a more or less "voluntary" means by which They may re-enslave mankind and, hopefully, bring a lasting peace to the planet Earth.

Before You all roll your eyes out of your heads, hear me out.

It has been postulated that if one can't bring Mohammed to the mountain, then bring the mountain to him.

The main idea is to enlist You and your fellow Earth Pures to help spread the word of the "*New Earth Gospel.*"

The Celestials possess the technology to simultaneously project an enormous, partially obscured, worldwide image of a generic "**All-Father**", who shares traits with every man, woman and child on Earth. Some will swear it's Jesus. Some will declare it's the face of the Buddha. Others will attest to seeing Muhammad, but most will insist that it is the actual face of God Himself.

He would telepathically speak to them in their native tongues about His return and the peaceful, bountiful world He is there to help create.

Any who outright oppose or attempt to attack Him will be immediately brought to their knees, and the rest are expected to quickly acquiesce and abandon their old ineffectual, dead religions, for Our new and undeniably certifiable **One World Religion**.

Cloaked Greys and other Celestial Pures will control the weather from above. They will defuse hurricanes and tornadoes. They will "seed" the clouds where rain is needed and move them to avoid floods. They will bring water to the deserts as we plant crops wherever they are needed. They will extinguish forest fires and end hunger.

Our job will be to supervise the rebuilding of the cities to withstand earthquakes and floods, and through mandatory nutritional guidance, bring an end to obesity. We will end unemployment and reduce stress. Every father and mother will be able to feed their children while resting assured that each child will receive an exemplary education.

If You so desire, You and your fellow Earth Pures could all become respected Apostles or religious leaders Who would no longer have to hide Your abilities because they would be deemed newly bestowed upon You by God Himself.

All guidance and worship would come from and through You. Non-pures would finally have confirmation of their devout faith as they watch their societies blossom, their weapons rust and their families thrive.

We will set the new course for humanity's progress as We abolish petty hatred, racism, envy, sloth, greed and class warfare.

Worldwide resources will be shared, and everyone will be made to work together in harmony to achieve an eventual Heaven on Earth.

No work will be too hard and no sacrifice too great, on their parts, to achieve *Our* goals. There is practically nothing mankind cannot and would not achieve with Us in control and them voraciously and willingly doing Our bidding.

"God" will have returned with fire in His hypnotic eyes and an authoritative assertiveness in His voice that commands unquestioned and complete obedience. And they will listen, and they will prosper, and We will have finally resumed Our rightful status on this planet Earth!

Russia: Bravo!

Britain: Hear, hear!

Washington: Brilliant! I love it! I love you!

Peru: That's it! I'm leaving my husband for you! Take me now, right here!

Israel: I love the concept…but it will never work.

CHAPTER 4

HUMAN VS. NATURE

China: What the hell do you mean it will never work? Why not?

Israel: Because, like them, We're Human.

Japan: Why in the hell should that matter? It sounds like the perfect plan. Everybody wins!

Israel: That's actually part of the problem. You see, Human Beings are competitive by nature. They have an irrational need to feel superior to others. And that applies to Us too.

Sooner or later there's going to be a power grab where one of Us wants to rise to the top as the head honcho and make other Pures bow down to Him or Her. We can't help Ourselves, We're made that way. That's exactly what happened before. Pures ended up killing Their own family members to gain stature and become more powerful. We jealously resented each other's accomplishments and sabotaged each other's efforts.

Pures love to think that We're a lot better than We actually are, but Our nature as Human Beings is to be self-sabotaging. We're self-destructive. We're self-abusive. We've got an innate mean streak and a survival-based selfishness to match. We hate being looked down upon, and sooner or later We're going to organize against the Celestials and tell Them to go back to Hell and leave Our planet to Us.

India: He's absolutely right. But not only that. Some Earth Pures have developed one heck of a conscience, and sooner or later a few are bound to crack.

You forget that many Earth Pures have fathered or given birth to Taints and Mutes Themselves. And if They haven't personally, then They have brothers, sisters, children or cousins who have.

It's only a matter of time before the truth slips out and the whole big "All-Father" lie comes crashing down.

Then the Mutes will hate and resent Us, and We will end up going even deeper undercover than We already are. We will finally be exposed and identifiable. There will be posters with Our faces and names on them. Mutes outnumber Us by an estimated 200,000 to one or more. Even with Our "powers" and Our superior intellects, We would be doomed.

Ethiopia: You know, the more I think about it, the less it sounds viable. Human Beings always find a way to screw things up. There would be conspiracy theories abounding before God's face even left the sky. Mutes would devote a corner of a closet in their homes to continue to worship their own long-dead "God"… "just in case". The proverbial "golden calf" business would go through the roof.

If history has taught Us nothing else, it has taught Us that Non-pures are not rational. They take life-threatening, mind-destroying drugs for a temporary high that oftentimes puts their very lives at risk. They will sacrifice their livelihoods and the well-being of their very own families for a quick fix or a cheap thrill.

They betray each other on a whim, and some would sell their own mothers for a dollar. They zealously peddle each other poison wrapped in plastic bags and distilled in glass bottles. They sell their very souls along with their sacred bodies for money.

They must truly hate themselves.

They are weak and unreliable. They buy things they can't afford, steal if the opportunity presents itself, cheat if they think they can get away with it, eat themselves into poor health, and lie for the hell of it.

Their pride will eventually motivate them to intentionally obliterate Heaven just to make some frivolous point. Many of them apparently like living in Hell, because they've either created their own version of it, or have grown inexplicably comfortable languishing in it.

They defile their magnificent bodies with tattoos and piercings and commit unthinkable sexual acts that are unnatural or abhorrent and cannot possibly be pleasurable.

Rome: I actually walked in on a Cardinal molesting a child once. And the Church protected him. I've seen the clergy sit around and talk about how stupid their parishioners are to give them so much of their hard-earned money.

I've seen them spit in the holy water and piss on the Church steps in a drunken stupor.

I've seen the bodies of infants buried by their Nun mothers beneath the Church.

I've witnessed a homosexual orgy in a suite inside the Domus Sanctae Marthae (Saint Martha's House) in the Vatican City. I have seen holy men defecate in holy places, and give Jesus Christ the finger. It won't work. Peace would never be sustainable because Human Nature won't allow it. We're our own worst enemy, and we will always desecrate perfection, because it reminds us too much of just how permanently, disgustingly and innately flawed we are.

Washington:	Native Americans, among others, have been trying to tell the world for many years that Humans are the main cause of nature's imbalance on our planet. Our protests have fallen on deaf ears. Mankind has chosen to continue to pollute and poison our world for profit. **Global Warming** and **Climate Change** are just politically inspired jokes to some of them.

Many understand the nightmare they are creating for generations to come, but they seemingly don't care at all. They believe it will be some future generation's problem to solve when the time comes, but by then the Earth will already have begun to strike back in insidious ways.

The Red People have already noted the beginning of the end with the melting ice caps, the unusually hot and cold weather, the droughts, floods and devastating hurricanes; they bear vigilant witness to the rising temper of Nature's wrath.

Sit there and smile if you choose, but I promise you, the Earth itself will have the last laugh.

China: At the present rate of population growth, the Earth will be overburdened by the turn of the next century. Many people, in their feigned ignorance and blatant arrogance, still believe that having a large family is their God-given birthright and a ticket to immortality. But the consequences of unchecked growth will be worldwide famine, plague, war and ultimately a greatly diminished dystopian way of life for generations to come.

We must hold population growth down before we find ourselves fighting over a lack of space, resources and tolerance. Having more than two to three children is both patently selfish and foolishly ill-advised. The Earth is quickly reaching a crisis point where it will no longer be able to sustain such unabated human expansion.

When the selfish desires of a few threaten to jeopardize the future of the many, then measures must be taken. This is no longer the seemingly inexhaustible world of Our Forefathers.

Earthkind may well be incapable of becoming collectively responsible for our actions. We choose to act as if our self-imposed tribulations will somehow take care of themselves without our global commitment to solve them. "I" has always been more important than "we" for the vast majority of "us."

Japan: We recently learned that when the nuclear genie gets out of the bottle, it can be extremely difficult to put him back in. Every precaution must be taken to avoid future nuclear incidents and accidents at all costs. Advancements should not be made at the expense of precaution and an obstinate determination to preserve a life-sustaining environment. Recklessly pursued progress will eventually result in adverse setbacks. Sometimes shortcuts are the predictable pathway to disaster.

Britain:	I'd still like to believe that it could work if we'd just be honest with them. It truly would be a win/win situation.

But there's another part of me that says that their penchant for distrusting anything and anyone that is different will drive them to rebel against Us with cries for the freedom to continue to suffer in their own squalid sense of self-determination. They would rather die hypothetically "free" than to live as healthy, happy slaves. As if we Human Beings could ever sustain happiness.

There is something inside of us that loves to complain and find fault with every little thing we see or that somebody says. We let every little faux pas get under our skin.

One of the most intrinsic traits to be found in human nature is dissatisfaction. Nothing ever seems to be quite good enough, and everything, no matter how admirable, can still be improved upon.

Jealousy is a human staple. We thrive on it. We take a swig of it every day just to remind ourselves that we aren't all that we can be, and that others aren't all that they think they are.

Our innate ability to dislike others can sometimes rival the inborn sense of self-dissatisfaction that we cannot seem to escape from. I'm too fat; you're too skinny. I hate my hair; your butt is too big. You're not as smart as you think you are; I wish I had a better memory. You're so vain; I'm so worthless. He's too smart for his own good; I'm an idiot.

Earth Humans like to get high or drunk to supposedly forget their problems, but instead, they are actually trying to tiptoe that razor-thin line between acceptable and unacceptable behavior, because they've been led to believe that that is where the "fun" is to be found.

On the other hand, apparently wisdom is an almost valueless commodity that is gained purely by chance, rather than by any applied effort to achieve or enhance it.

Wisdom, it seems, should be avoided at all costs because it is the ultimate "buzzkill."

Common sense is a liability to some who would rather stumble drunkenly through life, erroneously believing that deep insight may be garnered while one is arguably out of one's natural mind or otherwise chemically impaired.

If asked if they'd like to go to Heaven, there are sadly those who would inquire as to whether or not there will be beer there.

If Humans truly wanted to go to Heaven, they'd set about finding ways to create it right here on Earth. But they don't truly want Heaven, because it sounds too restrictive and unavoidably boring; and Humans thrive on constant drama. It is, seemingly, their most eagerly anticipated reason to get up in the morning.

Russia: You are right, of course, but there is another obvious major difference between Pures and the rest of the Humans. Pures have never quite understood nor embraced the allure of the gamble.

Many Sub-pures and Mutes like to gamble with their money, and when they win, most of them squander it all away in very little time. Easy come, easy go, as they say.

They gamble with their health by overeating disgustingly unhealthy foods and drinking copious amounts of liquid poisons. Others gamble by taking steroids or other neurologically damaging substances.

They gamble with their jobs by inattentively doing subpar or habitually sloppy work or by stealing from their workplace. Some come in when they feel like it or lie about suffering from ailments that they don't in fact have. Some spend half of their workday playing on the Internet or texting their friends.

Some gamble with their sanity by taking illicit drugs. Others gamble with their freedom by aligning themselves with groups of anarchists and hate groups who stand around spouting slogans of racial pride or the rhetoric of racist bigotry.

Some ceaselessly inundate their minds with visions of disgusting acts of pornography or relish in witnessing acts of violence and wanton mayhem.

Some gamble with their lives by driving drunk or by jumping out of airplanes and skiing down perilous ski slopes. Others, by climbing mercilessly unforgiving mountains or unnecessarily seeking confrontations with deadly species of wildlife.

It is clear to me that many humans don't feel alive unless they are cheating death.

Egypt: Like I said, we should just walk away. We don't have the moral justification to kill them all, and trying to change them is undoubtedly a fool's errand. They would have to want to change, and mankind's world history is strewn with countless examples of their fragile egos dictating an almost illogical resistance to accepting the help of others to bring about positive changes in their collective.

Non-pures are tragically, if not fatally, unbalanced, to put it mildly. But I truly don't think they realize that about themselves. Their insecurities have made them both cautiously paranoid and predictably careless at the same time. They repeatedly seek to defy all reasonable odds, at the expense of their personal and communal well-being, by rejecting any semblance of common sense.

They are self-defeating, excuse-making, sympathy-seeking misfits. They recklessly set themselves up for failure and then blithely blame life for being demonstrably unfair.

The level of hypocrisy they exhibit daily is astounding! They can easily point out the innumerable faults in others while obliviously ignoring the fact that they themselves possess many of the same exact negative traits. They are psychologically damaged little spirit/souls trying to make uncommon sense of a world they deem to be unnecessarily harsh and cruel.

Animals on this planet live in a constant state of paranoia because there is always some predator out there threatening their existence; but Humans fear each other far more than they do any other species. They fear each other and they don't trust each other; and I fear that they will never trust that We would ever have their best interests at heart. So, maybe We *should* just walk away and leave them at their own spurious mercy.

Peru: The man's got a point, but I for one have too much to lose by just walking away. Why should I give up all of my holdings and leave them to a bunch of ill-mannered, brain-damaged, unkempt, uncouth, uneducated rock worshippers?

Even I must admit that trying to tame the irrationally unreliable beast that is humanity, would probably end up being a waste of time in the long run. However, We could encourage additional mining and the stripping of natural resources that may be appreciated on the home planet when We get there. I mean, why should We pack up and leave Earth flat broke or empty-handed?

Australia: True, but the Celestials would prefer to set up trade agreements with them, and pay them, rather than fight them for their resources. They believe that mankind's insatiable greed alone would be a sufficient impetus to procure all of the ores and minerals They desire.

They would prefer to be granted leases to strip the Earth clean, using Their own efficiently superior mining technologies, rather than relying upon Earthkind's slow and cumbersome techniques. By the time the Non-pures figured out what was actually happening, the Celestials would have absconded with everything They wanted and more.

If They leave, They plan on being heavily compensated for Their extensive investment of time and expended resources, and They'll be more than happy to leave Earthkind to try to clean up the egregiously depleted mess They leave behind.

If, as predictably expected, They obtain Earthkind's cooperation, They have calculated that it will only take Them two to three centuries to literally and figuratively suck this planet dry.

Washington: Why do you keep saying They? If there is going to be a mass exodus, I plan on taking my family and getting the heck off of this whirling Hell hole of a planet, with the departing Celestials. I'm not about to stay down here with these reprehensible oafs.

Australia: You may not have a choice.

Which brings Us to the next part of my divulging.

My Father is a Celestial. Therefore, I have been offered an exit visa that would permit me to return to His home planet if a final Leaving or Departure is decided upon.

The rest of you, however, have been deemed unfit for reintegration on any of the home planets.

Rome: What exactly is that supposed to mean? I've done my time. I have remained true to all Pure ethics and customs. I have not defiled my body. I have honored my marriage. I have never been high or intoxicated. I have stayed away from the influences of their decadent cultures. I have been a loyal soldier and a trustworthy ally to the Celestials. I have earned my right to abandon this feces-laden waste of a Pure's time and energy!

I should not be punished just because I happen to have been born on this god-infested planet. I am just as pure as any Pure floating around off planet. I will **demand** an exit visa!

Britain: Hear, hear!

Washington: You got that damn right!

Peru: Something told me They were going to try to screw Us over!

Israel: If They won't take me off this planet, then They won't be taking any of our resources either. We have the damn bomb and we'll use it!

India: A million curses upon Them! I am not some damned untouchable, and I refuse to be treated like one!

Ethiopia: I figured as much. I have Mute family members, and no matter what We ultimately decide, I cannot see myself abandoning them.

Russia: We're totally screwed if We sit back and permit Them to suck this planet dry and then just fly away and strand Us here. I will either be granted an appeal or...

Australia: Or what?

Russia:	Or **war**, goddamn it! Just let Them try to land and see what happens! My father, his father, and his father before him were all warriors. I am not afraid to fight or to die! I will defend my planet to my last breath! *Who is with me?*
All:	*I am!* *We all are!* *They will never get away with this!* *They don't know Who They're messing with!* *Earth Pures unite!*
Australia:	And therein lies the problem. We're Earthborn. I can't leave my mother and my family behind. I'd miss them too much.

I can't be stoic and dispassionate. None of Us can. We're Earthborn, and like it or not, Our spirit/souls are tied to this planet. We love Our home. We just don't love some of the people living on it.

Let's face it, We are now more like the Mutes than We are like the Celestials.

When I speak to my Father, I realize that I cannot relate to the way He sees life. And He has never mentioned the word love to me as an Earth father might do to his son. There are no embraces or familial warmth. There is a dispassionate void where His heart ought to be.

I know He cares for me, but He doesn't laugh at my jokes like all of You do. He just doesn't get them, or me.

Don't get me wrong. He is a brilliant, kind, caring Human Being, but in many of the ways that really matter, He isn't Us. And We aren't Them. At least, not anymore.

The Celestials fear that We and Our families will take the infused insanity of the earth, that We have been swimming in since the day We were born, and export that madness back to the home planets, where We will inevitably plant the seeds of sedition and anarchy. And They are right.

We don't *think* like Them anymore. We don't *feel* like Them anymore. We don't know how to swallow Our hopes and desires and individualism, and become a good, cooperatively complacent citizen who only sees the Us and not the Me.

We are Earth Pures. And We need to learn to be proud of that, even if They are not.

Let Us take a break. I'll see You all in twenty minutes.

Help yourselves to one of these Nouri-tablets provided by my Father.

CHAPTER 5

LIFE SENTENCES

Australia: May I have everyone's attention please.

I have some mixed news to share with you.

My contact inside the Free Earth Movement has just informed me that they are now in the building, and have already been to the suite We previously occupied. They presently believe that We have vacated the premises and are considering a termination of their agenda.

He'll contact me again soon to let me know what decision they've come to. In the meantime, We are safe behind these reinforced steel doors in this windowless room. They should not be able to locate Us now that We have disposed of their tracking devices.

It seems that everyone has calmed down considerably.

Japan: These Nouri-tablets are delicious. Mine tastes a little like strawberries and baked chicken.

Russia: Really? Mine tastes more like steak and grape juice… but not quite.

Peru: I've got…I think it's pineapple and barbecued ribs. I will gladly pay for a few thousand boxes of these. Be sure to ask your Father on my behalf.

Washington: How do They get the sip of orange juice inside the dry tablet?

Australia: Ms. Peru. I seriously doubt that my Father can or will attempt to satisfy your request, but I shall ask Him if I'm given the chance.

Mr. Washington. I have no idea how the tablets are made, but I look forward to having one every time I visit the mothership.

It is my rudimentary understanding that much of the flavor is harvested from select body parts surgically removed from cattle, chickens, goats, sheep and other animals.

Now, if I may… Why is everyone so calm all of a sudden? When I stepped out, the room was ready to go to war.

Britain: Japan reminded us that there was still one scenario left. Edification; a sharing of Celestial technology and philosophies. It's either that, or these Nouri-tablets are drugged. Not that I care.

Australia:	You may have something there. They have the same calming effect on me.
	It has occurred to me that We beat Sub-pures and Non-pures up pretty badly in Our last segment. We blamed them for all of Our ills and could not seem to find a single redeeming quality among them.
	Did you know that Australia-born **Terrance Tao** is a so-called Mid- to High-level **Taint**, as were **Benjamin Franklin** and **Thomas Jefferson**?
Washington:	So were **Thomas Edison, Alexander Graham Bell, Benjamin Banneker, George Washington Carver, Frederick Douglass** and the **Wright Brothers**.
Rome:	As were **Archimedes, Pythagoras, Socrates, Aristotle, Voltaire, Leonardo DaVinci, Giordano Bruno, Galileo, Ptolemy, Mozart,** and **Michelangelo**.
India:	Let us not forget **Mother Teresa, Mahatma Gandhi, Sage Agastya** and **Srinivasa Ramanujan**.
Japan:	Or **Emperor Meiji, Oda Nobunaga** and **Kōnosuke Matsushita**.
Egypt:	How about **Hannibal** and **Amenhotep III?**
Peru:	**Simon Bolivar, Evita Peron,** and **Jose Marti**.
Britain:	**Sir Isaac Newton, Robert Boyle, Nostradamus, Joan of Arc, Leif Erikson, Michael Faraday,** and **John Lennon**.
Ethiopia:	**Cleopatra, Shaka Zulu, Aesop** and **Nelson Mandela**.
Russia:	**Rasputin, Ivan the Great, Alexander the Great, Mozart, Houdini, Leibniz, Copernicus, Beethoven, Tesla, Tsiolkovsky** and **Wernher von Braun**.
China:	**Preah Pisnokar, Confucius, Marco Polo** and **Genghis Khan**.
Israel:	**John the Baptist, King David, Albert Einstein,** and **Sammy Davis Jr.!**
Australia:	See, that wasn't hard at all.
	Now let Us each try to identify one trait that We like about Non-pures that makes them worth saving and possibly makes them worthy of Our help to reach the next level of their collective maturity.
Peru:	I want to go first because I want to discuss the pink elephant in the room.
	Apparently nobody wants to admit it, but Mutes need Our help to get anything

done. Pures have always been the catalyst for most of the great achievements on the planet Earth.

Now, I know that some of you are in denial, but when the initial Drops were first made on this planet, all but a few Mutes were treated as free men. The exceptions being those who were immediately put to mining gold.

Thousands of years later, when the New Celestials took over and largely re-enslaved the Mutes, we got great civilizations like the Inca, Maya, Aztec, Romans, Egyptians, Chinese, East Indians and the British.

But where freedom reigned and the Overseers left the Mutes to their own devices, they sat on their asses and got high. Look at the Aborigines, the North American Indians and most Africans.

They were free to *not* achieve. Name one great invention or innovation to come from any of them. Well? That's my point. If the Celestials had not intervened, Humans on Earth might very well still be living in caves.

Now, having said that, and knowing that I may have hurt a few feelings, I openly admit that I love Mute **Music**. That, by itself, is so special and speaks to the heart and soul of Humanity so eloquently, that no species in the universe could see fit to snuff out a people capable of creating such beauty.

What other species on this entire planet plays instruments and creates new songs?

And singing? Singing is mankind's gift to the cosmos. May it reverberate throughout, forever.

I love Salsa, Rhythm and Blues, Reggae, Indian music, African rhythms, Classical music, Hawaiian, Caribbean, Pop, Rock, Jewish music, Russian music, Asian music, British music, Arabic music, Irish music, Country music…. Obviously, I just plain love music.

I listen to it all day long; from the moment I wake up to the moment I go to sleep. Music can make me laugh and it can make me cry.

Music exposes the human condition and touches something deep inside of us all. Music can be a time machine that takes our minds and hearts back to the places and people of our past. Music is beauty and beauty should always be preserved.

Mutes deserve to live, if only to keep making music.

Washington: **Art** has the same effect on me. In fact, I'm an avid collector.

Art is an avenue into the soul of man. Art can provide us with a glimpse into Heaven and allow us a peek into Hell. Art can express our fears and reveal our dreams. It can be wonderful and frightening. It can be literal or pure fantasy.

Art can bring beauty to desolate places and express complex Human feelings such as rage or love with a brush stroke. Art can edify or demean, soothe or irritate, elevate the spirit or evoke feelings of hopelessness.

Art is man's way of recreating the world as it was, as we see it now, as we wish it could be, or hope it will never be.

Art can take us across the universe or to the depths of our inner insecurities.

I can sit and gaze at the same painting for hours as it draws me in and takes me away to a more beautiful place that quiets my anguish and reassures my hopes.

I love art, and the people who make art. Art should never die, and nor should those who so lovingly create it.

India: For me it's **Philosophy**.

Great minds and great wisdom turn me on. Who would have thought that Taints and Mutes were even capable of such introspective depth?

Humans are the only species on Earth who can share thoughts of things that never were and may never be. We are the sole purveyors of the "What if." We massage the truth as we believe it to be and force others to contemplate and ultimately question their own values and beliefs.

Unlike religion, philosophy offers little certainty and yet brings with it increased insight into oneself and how one molds reality out of our own unique perspective.

Philosophy exposes biases and challenges traditions. It questions our basic beliefs and widens our narrow-mindedness. It encourages contemplation and rewards us with refined insight.

Philosophy is the pathway to enlightenment.

Philosophy should be the new religion.

And those capable of contemplative insight into the universe and the nature of "*being*" itself... deserve to live forever.

Ethiopia: **Dance**.

What is it about dance that can free a man's soul from inhibition? That allows him to express joy through movement and beauty with a gesture or a pirouette? That evokes sadness and remorse in others? That can bring a depressed spirit/soul back to life? That speaks without words, screams without sound, cries without tears, laughs without smiling?

Dance is beauty personified. Dance is the expression of life as only Humans can express it.

I don't know why it is only man who has learned to express joy and pain in a universally understood medium, but this world is a better place because man dances.

We dance because we can. We dance because we must. We dance because our very souls want release.

We dance because it is who we are, behind closed doors, far from judging eyes, in our own private little world... we dance.

No species in the universe can deny that such beauty must be preserved.

Britain: All Humans, but especially Non-pures and Sub-pures, have the inexplicable capacity to **Sympathize and Empathize**.

At first glance this may not seem significant, but in reality it is one of the traits that best defines our very Humanity.

It is one thing for me to worry about myself and my pain, but for me to be concerned about *your* pain when I don't even know you...is a glimpse at divinity.

Why do we cry just because someone else is crying? How is it that *we* feel loss just from being in the presence of someone else who has experienced the loss of a loved one we'll never chance to meet?

Why do we feel joy as others celebrate? Why does their happiness add to our own?

The ability to share feelings with or without words is beyond special. A facial expression, watering eyes, an inflection in the voice, the hanging of the head, or a single sigh, is enough to garner an understanding hug from another.

We laugh together, we cry together. We laugh while we're crying, we cry while we're laughing, and we laugh simply because we are crying.

Your tears bring my tears. Your pain causes me pain. Your sadness brings me sadness.

Your wound makes me shudder inside. And that means we're all connected. And that makes us special. That makes us beautiful.

The capacity to sympathize and empathize puts Humans at the very top of the "Right to Live" list.

Israel: **The Will to Survive.**

When all hope is gone. When defeat and death are all but certain. When buried beneath the rubble of life with no chance for escape, with the waters of anguish rising and the world growing silent…the spark remains. The Human spirit prevails.

We reach deep and cultivate hope where only despair exists; and we survive. Against all odds, against all expectations, against all doubt and understanding, somehow, some way, we hang on. We endure. We refuse to give in to abject hopelessness and common sense. With our final breath we seek to grab hold of immortality and spit in the face of death.

You cannot defeat me, you cannot have my soul! I am a Human Being and therefore will defy you beyond the end. Even in the darkness. Even in the pits of Hell itself, my spirit/soul will endure until divine forgiveness is granted and eternal peace is realized.

I may not know what God or gods exist in the outside universe, but I know of the one that dwells within me. And I shall not betray him. We shall fight together… and endure.

The right to live must pay homage to the Will to Survive.

Japan: **Creative Imagination**, by which I mean the Human capacity to create a new reality from an idea. To bring a concept to life in the form of a movie, a play or a video game.

What other species on Earth can create an alternate reality? What else can make the unbelievable believable. Our minds are capable of taking bits and pieces of reality and somehow shape them into something we've never seen before.

Unique cities and landscapes leap from our creative minds. Creatures are born from the amalgamation of inspiration.

The impossible becomes possible. The unknowable becomes discernible. The unthinkable becomes reality and reality becomes the dream.

The power to create exists within us. It is visceral, it is innate. It can be seen in the smallest child at play and in the eldest of us learning to compensate for their fading abilities.

Innovation is the mother of adaptation.

Our world has drastically changed with the introduction of the microchip. But in reality it is merely a new tool to be used to create the existence we aspire to, out of the one we inherited.

The boundaries of Human prosperity are inextricably tied to our creative imaginations.

Extinguishing the Human spark of creation, would be like killing Nature itself.

China: I would say it's our **Sense of Humor**.

What other species on Earth has the innate ability to laugh at itself? I mean, I fully acknowledge that some animals *seem* to laugh at others, but we literally laugh at ourselves.

Sometimes we make stupid mistakes or the words don't come out just right or we thoroughly embarrass ourselves in front of others…and we laugh.

We have even developed the art of tickling other's funny bones with our words or actions. We can bring each other to tears with a joke or a mental mishap.

Our facial expressions alone seem almost endless, diverse and universal; and we have learned that a single look can cause others to collapse in a fit of uncontrollable laughter where breath becomes an unreachable commodity.

The Human sense of humor is undoubtedly unique. What we find funny may not apply to any other species, but it is a gift we give to ourselves and to one another.

It should not be taken for granted; rather, it should be cherished. It's just one of the many things that make mankind so uniquely special.

And if you don't agree, then just try to imagine this world without laughter.

Rome: I am always astonished by mankind's **Nurturing nature**.

Most species hold and cuddle and show signs of love towards one another within their own species, but we feel the need to rescue and nurse back to health, animals that would seek to kill us if given the chance.

This is an almost irrational trait we possess. We will eat a chicken and then turn around and rescue a baby sparrow, and try to keep it alive until it can fly away.

We pick up stray animals and give them a loving home. We feed them, bathe them, shelter them from harm, and learn to love them, even when there is no gratitude or reciprocation.

I don't even pretend to understand why anyone else's baby is afforded the same love and compassion as our own. We will sacrifice our own lives to save the child of a stranger. We will adopt and raise another's child as our own.

We will comb their hair, caress their backs, wipe their mouths and rock them to sleep. We want them to feel the love we instinctively feel inside.

We want all those we love to feel how much we care, and how their well-being is important to us. We want the best for them even if all we can afford to give them is hope. We want them to feel safe. We want them to know that somebody cares.

I'm not sure where it comes from, but our nurturing nature sets us apart from all others. And that is a trait too precious to ever lose.

Egypt: It's **Architecture** that floats my boat. And I don't mean just the amazing pyramids.

Mankind is the only species on Earth that literally alters the landscape by attempting to build structures that are not only functional but also beautiful and awe-inspiring.

When a bird builds a nest, it is usually constructed in the very same way every other bird of its species builds a nest. Any innovation is usually accidental, and there is never any attempt to impress any other animal unless it's a potential mate.

Animals seek functionality above all else. Not so with Humans. We love to make a defining statement. We want to scream out that I was here and look what I've accomplished!

At times functionality is not the least bit important. Sometimes it is beauty alone that inspires and defines the architecture.

Practicality can be totally excluded from the design and schematics We want to astound. We want to awe. We want to impress. We want to stretch the limits of possibility and defy nature to match our grandeur and engineering expertise.

"If you build it, They will come."

Well, we're going to keep on building it, because it's who we are and it's what we do.

Russia:	Are you kidding me? No one said **Food**!

Only Humans can find a dozen different ways to prepare the same ingredient. All other animals know nothing about cooking. They eat what they find. They eat the same foods their ancestors ate with no derivations or innovations.

We, on the other hand, never stop experimenting with different tastes and more exotic combinations. We can use the same fruit in a hundred different ways.

It's no wonder the world keeps growing fatter!

The preparation of food is one of mankind's greatest achievements. And Mutes may be better at it than anyone else. I think their taste buds must be enhanced to compensate for other things they do not do so well, because when I sit down in a fine restaurant, my mouth begins to water with anticipation and my eyes grow large with wonder at the exquisite meal they lay before me.

Yes, I am fat. But I do not care! The bigger I am the more I can eat, and eating is what it is all about.

Eating is both a necessity and a pleasure. Food is what we make it; and boy, do we know how to make it!

Hand me another Nouri-tablet. I just made myself hungry again!

Australia:	It's **Love**. All of you have said exactly that, in your own way.

We love the things we talked about. We cherish them. We admire those traits we find within ourselves; meaning within *all* of mankind.

Admit it, We did nothing to deserve being born as Pures. We just woke up one day and there We were.

And Sub-pures and Non-pures did nothing to deserve their plights. Like Us they are just playing the hand fate dealt them. They're just doing the best they can with what they've got, or weren't given.

We may be able to do a lot of things better than they are capable of, but the one thing We can't do… is *out-love* them.

Their capacity to love even exceeds Our own.

Their love is irrational, unfettered, inexhaustible, all-encompassing and contagious.

As flawed as they are, their capacity to love is unmatched and, indeed, Divine. If We were looking for God, I think We'd recognize Him there, in the love Humanity has in its wondrous soul.

They love Us. They may not know who We are, but We can see it in their smiles, feel it in their embraces, and hear it in their voices.

And if We'd climb down off of Our high horses, We'd learn to love them too. Flaws and all. Just as We love Our own undeveloped children.

Some of You began this Summit expressing your allegiance to the Edification camp. I sense that some of Us might just join You when it's time to vote.

The Celestials have heretofore been very reluctant to share Their advanced Celestial Technology with Earthkind. Most of Them feel that this would be like handing the keys to a race car to a small child who lacks a sufficient understanding of the ramifications of his or her careless actions.

Advancing Earthkind to the next level assumes that controlling or improving their day-to-day struggles with food supplies, medicinal needs, wealth distribution, and spiritual or mental concerns, would ultimately lead to worldwide peace and enhanced maturity.

We would be employed to help implement all technological and societal changes, but without the potential risks that exposure would bring. They still wouldn't know who We *really* are.

Those who support this step have been insisting that Earthkind's insanely unbalanced and irrational behaviors are causally connected to their struggle to survive.

Earthkind has been indoctrinated to believe that all of those who do not resemble them physically or religiously, are a threat to their very existence. History has shown us all that they may in fact be right. Right, because they have inadvertently proven to each other that those threats can be real.

This well-warranted paranoia is all-pervasive and deeply ingrained in the Human psyche. And regrettably it is also to be found in the psyches of the Celestials Themselves, Who see Earthkind as both a potentially valuable ally, as well as a potentially viable threat.

There are many accounts of the rise of one civilization ultimately causing the downfall or demise of another. This is most disheartening when it is shown that the now besieged civilization was, in fact, instrumental in inspiring or cultivating their newly declared enemy's military prowess.

Sooner or later, independence is always sought after and fought for.

Celestials believe that without Their strictly controlled intervention, Earthkind will use their newly found gifts against each other for nationalistic or religiously motivated gain, even at the expense of finally establishing an enduring peace and universal prosperity.

Reportedly, an emissary named **Valiant Thor** was sent by The Celestial High Council to speak with President Eisenhower in 1957, but his attempt to ameliorate mankind's push towards inevitable destruction was met with staunch resistance from America's military leaders, who rebuffed his peaceful agenda.

The Celestial Pures have since openly conceded that They do not fully understand Earthkind, which includes Us. That is why They are deferring to Our better judgment to best direct the vicissitudes of Their continued involvement, if any.

Hopefully We won't let Pure pride stand in the way of doing what We know in Our hearts We *should* do.

Are there any further comments any of You would like to add at this time?

Russia: I came in wanting to beat the Mutes into submission, and I still have my reservations, but I like the **New Religion** option the best. If no one else agrees, then I might sign on to the idea of sharing limited Celestial Tech with them in the hopes that they will see the light and change their ways. But I seriously doubt it.

Rome: Okay, okay, maybe We shouldn't kill them all, but helping them take their madness to the stars just doesn't sit well with me. I say We **Emancipate** them, try to limit our mining agreements with the Celestials, and hold our breath that it doesn't come to war.

Egypt: Let's try the **Edification** thing, and if it doesn't work, let's just give up and leave them alone.

Japan: Now I am convinced, more than ever, that through **Edification** We can change them with the verifiable promise of a better way; and convince them to stop warring and start cooperating with each other.

Washington: You guys have a lot more faith in them than I do. Instead of exterminating them all, I say We just put the hammer down, **Re-enslave** them, and make them do what We tell them to do. We can try that New Religion thing first, but I seriously doubt that it will work.

Israel: I've done a 180. I say We try **Edification**, but temper it with the threat of complete abandonment if they don't totally cooperate. Any push back, and We take Our toys and go home.

India: You forget that if the Celestials leave, They are going to leave Us here with these pathetic nuts. If I'm going to be stuck here, then I say We **Edify** them and hope they learn something useful before they screw things up and chase the Celestials away again.

China:	I still say we **Emancipate** them, and those of Us left here will just have to keep on doing what We've been doing. Maybe We can secure some of the mining rights and rack up some huge profits. I don't know about you, but I've got a family to feed.
	But look, if the majority of You want to try this sketchy Edification thing, I'm sure I can learn to turn it to my advantage.
Ethiopia:	I was leaning towards emancipation until you explained that We are to be left here. Now I am leaning towards **Edification**. We all stand to profit from that. It will be left up to Us Earth Pures to keep the Non-pures and Sub-pures from ruining it for everybody. I don't trust that they will behave themselves, but Our options are limited.
Peru:	Are You kidding me? You *know* they're going to turn on Us one day, and when they do they'll make You all regret that You've grown soft and idle-minded. Let's just **Re-enslave** them with a New Religion, and if that doesn't work, screw 'em. Nuke 'em! I really don't give a damn anymore.
	Those sons of bitches up there owe me a new planet, free of Mutes and Taints, and I'm going to hold Them to it. Let Me talk to Them. I can convince Them that We don't deserve to be abandoned here in Hell with a bunch of reprehensible, morally deprived demons.
	My family has been providing the Celestials with ore from Our mines for thousands of years, and this is the thanks that my family and I get?
	I'll be damned if They're going to strip this planet clean and leave my family here to rot! Let Me talk to Them!
	Are You guys listening through this damned transcorder? Don't start something You can't finish! I've got billions in assets and all the military connections I need to make Your lives miserable. Either put Us in control or get Us the Hell out of here!
Australia:	Sadly, you're making Their point for Them, and hopefully you haven't doomed Us all. It's emotional outbursts like that one that frightens Them most.
	If Earth Pures have abandoned wisdom for selfishness, then what hope is there for Earthkind as a whole?
	They heard you, but you may not care for Their response. You should hope that They have not been infected with the same self-centeredness you have displayed. Hope that They have remained bigger and better than We are. If not…then it may not matter what We decide here today.

They may determine us all to be non-redeemable, and pull the plug.

No help, and no hope for redemption. Your mouth may have compromised us beyond reconciliation. Let Us not forget, We can't *make* Them do anything. They have extended to Us Their ears, and claim to value Our counsel…and You've seen fit to threaten Them.

Peru: My deepest and sincerest apologies to You all. I take full responsibility for my thoughtless rantings. I've got a lot of soul-searching to do, and if I am left ostracized and despised by You, then it is no one's fault but my own.

I am officially announcing that I am going to vote for **Edification**, because I need to be reminded of who I am, and I could definitely use some of the psychological help the Celestials would afford us.

If You are still monitoring these proceedings, then know that I am finally beginning to acknowledge the errors in my way of thinking, and would very much like to toast to a continued relationship with Our Celestial Brothers.

All: Here, here!
          I agree!
          I can hardly wait!
          Let's get this party started!
          Bring on the motherships!

Australia: Ms. Peru, what is that on the bottom of your Starbucks cup? Let me see…

Damnit! It's another transmitter!

Peru: But I… It was that damned limo driver! I never should have let him go in and get my coffee for me. I could sense that he was up to something because he kept blocking me out. Now I know why. Do you think the Free Earthers are still in the building?

Australia: I don't know, but I'm about to find out!

Everyone keep your cool and wait until I get back!

Australia:	My contact is on the run. He has commandeered one of their vehicles and is being pursued as We speak. He couldn't say much, but he assured me that not only are they in the building, but when Ms. Peru lifted her cup, it was just enough for them to pinpoint Our location.
	He believes that they were monitoring his conversations with me, which is why they hadn't vacated the premises. It's my fault that they know We're still here.
	Ladies and gentlemen, prepare Yourselves for the wor…
	{The following account was added by a survivor immediately following the attack.}

The explosion that blew the steel doors off their hinges also served to disable the two Security men at the door.

Immediately Ms. Britain sprang into action.

Britain:	Mr. Japan, trade places with Mr. Washington. Ms. India: up there! Mr. Australia, behind me.
	I SAID BEHIND ME, GODDAMNIT! NOW!

Throwing her arms upwards and outwards as she cast her spell, the room quickly filled with a thick mist which all but completely obscured Their sight.

Rome:	I can't see a blasted thing!
Britain:	Neither can they. Heads down, NOW!

The first wave of the Free Earthers swept into the room, preceded by a barrage of automatic gunfire.

Britain:	Use Your inner eyes! We can do this!

Crossing her arms above her head and covering her face with her cape, was no deterrent to the dozen of bullets that sent her sprawling backwards and collapsing in a heap against the back wall.

As a bullet creased the top of his skull, no one saw Japan's attack, but they heard his blood-curdling scream, immediately followed by the truncated scream of his assailant.

Washington sprang into action, telekinetically sending two soldiers flying back against their fellow soldiers who were rushing through the entrance.

Suddenly the huge conference table in the middle of the room responded to Peru's gestures and flung itself forward, severing the spines of three of the opposition.

It was then that a device was tossed into the room which exploded, not with a concussive blast, but with an electrical charge.

Australia was sent screaming to the back of the room, where he crashed against the rear wall and fell lifelessly upon the floor.

Seeing this sent Russia into a rage. He grabbed the legs of a fallen soldier and began swinging him like a battle axe at his fellow soldiers, who were utterly stunned by his show of strength.

Their hesitation was all it took for China and Rome to rush forward, warding off the gunfire with their minds and engaging the soldiers in mind-to-hand combat.

India dropped down from the ceiling behind the encroaching soldiers and mentally yanked the helmets from three of their heads. As they turned to engage her, she spun upwards back into the mist, followed closely by sweeping gunfire.

This move opened them up to China's deadly chop to the throat of one, crushing his windpipe, as Rome sent the palm of his hand upward and into the nose of another of the soldiers standing before him, sending the bones and cartilage up into his brain.

Another wave of Free Earthers entered, firing wildly into the mist. One of the bullets found Rome's shoulder, causing him to stumble backward and ultimately hit the floor with a loud thud. Instantly a soldier was upon him, squeezing the trigger of his weapon before suddenly slumping to the floor.

Behind him stood Ethiopia with the soldier's still beating heart clutched in one hand while he extended his other hand to help Rome up off the floor.

Peru began waving her arms wildly as she sent chair after chair in the direction of the ducking and dodging soldiers. Out of nowhere India reappeared, just in time to come down, using her fists to cave in the skulls of the two soldiers who had trained their weapons on Peru.

Heeee-yaaaaaah!!

Japan's mental scream startled everyone in the room as his unbridled wrath cut a swath through the opposition.

This was followed by an additional wave of soldiers, screaming their own screams of desperation and resolve as they entered the room.

India: Try to pull their helmets off with your minds. Their helmets are shielding them from us.

Israel sprang to life and, closing his eyes, concentrated on the faint mental signatures of the soldiers in the room who dropped their weapons in a failed attempt to keep their helmets in place.

Ethiopia used the moment to send his elbows crashing through the skulls of two soldiers.

Russia, with the sweep of his hand, decapitated the next soldier coming through the door.

India grabbed the minds of two soldiers and sent mental spikes through them, permanently reducing them to brain-damaged vegetables.

Egypt leapt forward, too late to stop the first bullet that entered India's side, but not too late to put four of his fingers through the eye sockets of two soldiers, leaving them blind and writhing on the floor.

The final wave of twenty-plus soldiers rushed into the room, firing at will and sending all of the embattled Pures scrambling for the corners.

All but one.

The soldiers' screams could be heard throughout the building as they collapsed, grabbing their heads in a failed attempt to stop their brains from frying in their skulls.

And suddenly… there was silence.

The mist quickly began to dissipate as Australia stepped forward with Britain by his side.

Australia: I need a head count. Open Your minds to me.

              Britain, see to Rome's injury.

              Washington and Russia, see if You can secure the steel doors.

              India, do you require assistance?

India: Do you actually believe that one little bullet can take me out? I have already removed it and have already begun the healing process.

              Forgive me, but I must take a few moments to concentrate and meditate.

Australia: Peru?

Peru: My face is bleeding. I can stop the blood, but I know it's going to leave a permanent scar. Don't worry, I know a brilliant plastic surgeon.

Japan: Give me a moment to regain my Zen and repair my Karma. I lost myself somewhere in the battle. I will join China on the other side of the room.

Ethiopia: Ms. Britain, I thought you were dead. I saw you struck by many bullets.

Britain: This cape is bulletproof; it's made of Kevlar.

Ethiopia: But how did you know...

Britain: Because unlike most of you, I have fully developed my precognitive skills.

              Mr. Chairman, I have telekinetically extracted the bullet from Mr. Rome's shoulder, and I am now psychically healing the wound with His help.

Washington: You saved my life when you had me trade places with Japan. The bullet that grazed his skull would have buried itself inside my brain.

Britain: You're welcome. Anytime.

Egypt: I'm okay...thanks for asking.

Australia: You fought bravely. I would be honored to call you my friend.

Peru: As would We all. All of You guys surprised the Hell out of me! There were no wimps in this room!

              And, ladies...... I'm speechless.

China: Does that mean...

Peru: Speechless and still very much married.

Japan: You can't blame a guy for being persistent.

Australia: Ethiopia, China, Japan and Peru, I need You all to move the bodies of the soldiers into the back room.

              Mr. Japan, I'm sure you can make arrangements to have the soldiers' bodies discreetly removed from these premises after We have all safely left this airspace.

Japan: Not a problem. Consider it done.

Australia: Washington, Russia, Egypt and Israel, help me move the table and chairs back into place and reset this room.

Israel: What happened to you at the beginning of the battle? You collapsed.

Australia: They deployed some kind of a mini EMP (electromagnetic pulse) that temporarily knocked all of my enhancements offline. I had been temporarily rendered completely incapacitated and would not have survived the battle if Ms. Britain had not lain over me and protected me with her cape.

Rome: How did they know about your enhancements?

Australia: That *is* the question, isn't it?

India: It doesn't really matter. I just made my mind up. I want every one of those Mute bastards crucified.

Britain: You don't mean that.

Ethiopia: You can't possibly still expect Us to help these maniacs by sharing C.P. Tech with them so that they can use it against Us! They can all go to Hell!

Japan: Even I'm beginning to have my doubts. Screw 'em!

Australia: If everyone is through with their assigned tasks, could you please return to Your seats.

                It has become quite evident that We need to bring this Summit to a close.

                Ms. Britain, how are the two guards?

Britain: Not good. They're both still unconscious, but I don't think their concussions and broken bones are life-threatening.

Australia: Thank you, please return to your seat for now.

                Ladies and gentlemen, I would like to call this meeting back to order one final time.

Washington: As far as I'm concerned, you can call it over. I don't much care what They do to those lunatics.

Peru: Me either. But, given a choice, I want them all in chains. We should have known better than to think they were worth trying to save. The Pure Way is the only way.

                 We need to build a new Pure colony here on Earth that cannot be found by the Mutes. Even if it's a couple of miles under the ocean. Let the Celestials do whatever They want. I don't want anything else to do with this.

Britain: So, that's it then? We shirk our responsibility and walk away. We give up and We give in. We go into hiding for the rest of Our lives and condemn Our families to the same fate or worse.

                 I guess I was wrong.

China: Wrong about what?

Britain: Wrong about Us. I thought We were warriors. I thought We proved that today. I thought We were willing to fight and die for what We believe in. But I guess We don't really believe in anything anymore.

Russia: Why should We? We've been betrayed by the Celestials and attacked by the Mutes all on the same day.

Israel: He's right. Nobody wants Us.

Rome: I'm going to ask you again. How did they know about your enhancements?

Australia: And I'll tell you again, that I don't know.

Rome: Well, do you think your Father told the Free Earth Movement about them?

Australia: ……………..I'm not sure. I don't want to believe that He would do something like that to me.

                 Besides, that wouldn't make any sense. He's a first order Precog. He must have foreseen what might transpire here today, which is why He insisted that I have the enhancements installed.

Washington: Then how did they know? Could it have been someone aboard your Father's ship?

Japan: I've heard rumors for some time now that there are actually a few Celestial and Earth Pures working with the Free Earth Movement. That can't be true, can it?

India: Why would any Pure want to sabotage this Summit? It just doesn't make any sense.

Russia:	Counterterrorism tactics. We used them all the time during the cold war. You use propaganda to scare a third party into doing what you cannot openly do. You leak false information to them and sit back and watch the fireworks. It worked well with Iraq.
Israel:	Are you suggesting that there are Pures who turned the Mutes against Us, so that We'd turn against them? That's brilliant! The Mossad has been trying crap like that for years. And guess what? It works.
China:	So, You're saying We're being played? Someone told the Free Earthers that We were planning to either exterminate them all or re-enslave the Earth, and they were just trying to stop Us. Which is exactly what all of Us would have done.
Britain:	That means that those soldiers were just fighting for the lives of the people they loved. They were willing to die to remain free. But why would the Celestials want Us to condemn the Mutes?
Ethiopia:	For the ore and minerals. There are some Celestials who stand to make a tremendous profit by selling Earth's riches to other planets They have trade agreements with. Most of the ore wouldn't even be going to Humans on other planets.
Australia:	Ladies and gentlemen, We may, in fact, have just been played for fools. The helmets the soldiers were wearing to block out Our psychic attacks were Celestial Tech. So was the transmitter on Peru's cup and the EMP device. Rogue Celestials were definitely involved in today's assault. They thought that it was a win/win for Them. If the Free Earthers had slaughtered Us all, then Celestials like my Father would have been horrified and would have insisted on either destroying this planet or re-enslaving mankind. However, if We prevailed, They were sure that We would be enraged enough to vote for eradication, or re-enslavement at the very least, to exact Our retribution. The question is, are We going to give Them what They want, or are We going to show Them what happens when you try to screw over Earth Pures?
India:	But, what if it was just the Mutes attacking Us with gear they managed to buy on the Grey Market?
Egypt:	I hate being played for a fool. But can We take the chance that the Mutes won't turn on Us after We help them?

Ethiopia:	It may very well be the chance We *have* to take.
Britain:	We can always go into hiding, but I'd like to keep that option as a last resort.
	Just imagine what the Earth would look like after a hundred years of Celestial cooperation. Imagine what that could mean for Our families and Pure generations to come.
Washington:	You mean if the Mutes don't turn around and wipe Us all out.
India:	I'd like to see them try.
Australia:	I wouldn't. But, as Ethiopia said, that's the chance We may have to take.
	What happened here today speaks loudly as to Our dilemma. The Mutes meant to kill Us to save their own.
	The Celestials don't want Us. So, whatever decision We make has got to be in Our own best interest.
	To me that means that it comes down to Re-enslavement or Edification. Malevolence or Benevolence? That is the question before Us. And either way, it puts Us in control.
	Ultimately, the Celestials may not care what We decide. They may have made up Their minds to kill Us all and to strip the planet Earth barren. But We can't control that. We can only send Them a message telling Them what We have decided, and hope that They'll listen.
	Their response may come in a matter of days or decades.
Japan:	How are We going to tell Them anything? This transcorder has been smashed beyond repair.
Australia:	That device is a decoy.

I am the transcorder.

Today is Earth date December 21, 2012

Shall We vote?

{The following page had been redacted}

~~~~~~~~~~~~~~~~~~~~

Hy Shekdo

(The End)

Acknowledgments:

A special thank you to **Giorgio A. Tsoukalos & *Ancient Aliens*, Erich Von Daniken, Zecharia Sitchin, Wikipedia, Wikispaces, Wikimedia, **The Chart of Human Evolution by Bruce MacEvoy**, and all of the other **"Truth Pioneers"** who have preceded me.

PERMISSIONS

	Picture	page #	Source	
1.	Planet Earth	Cover	Shutterstock	129099683
2.	UFO/Flying Saucer	Cover	Shutterstock	52474045
3.	Stars	Cover	Shutterstock	172513382
4.	Anunnaki	11	Shutterstock	359927888
5.	Archangel Michael	13	Shutterstock	550762468
6.	Star Beings	14	Shutterstock	5701503002
7.	Wandjina	14	Shutterstock	1083175217
8.	Kakadu Cave Painting	15	Shutterstock	382037593
9.	Osiris and Isis	16	commons.wikipedia.org	Free for commercial use
10.	Akhenaten	17	110 pounds & counting	Free for commercial use
11.	Nefertiti	17	commons.wikipedia.com	Free for commercial use
12.	Tutankhamen	17	drapak.ca	Free for commercial use
13.	Baalbek	18	Shutterstock	5369096512
14.	Petra	18	Shutterstock	1030695769
15.	Kaaba	19	islam44.blogspot.com	Free for commercial use
16.	Pyramids at Giza	20	Shutterstock	173174633
17.	Great Sphinx at Giza	20	onexproof.deviant.art.com	Free for commercial use
18.	Imhotep	21	commons.wikipedia.org	Free for commercial use
19.	Filitosa Menhir	23	www.filitosa.fr	Free for commercial use
20.	The Minoans	24	Shutterstock/alltheropes.org	570469132 Free for com
21.	King Minos	25	commons.wikipedia.org	Free for commercial use
22.	Zeus	25	Shutterstock	459125665
23.	Theseus slays the Minotaur	26	commons.wikimedia.org	Free for commercial use
24.	Neptune/Poseidon	26	Shutterstock	1047510271
25.	Helios	27	commons.wikipedia.org	Free for commercial use
26.	UFO Battle Over Nuremberg	28	en.wikipedia.org	Free for commercial use
27.	Hagar Qim	28	Shutterstock	194479907
28.	Apollo	29	Shutterstock	713315764
29.	Delphi	29	Shutterstock	768491299
30.	Jimmu the Pure	30	commons.wikipedia.org	Free for commercial use
31.	Cetho Temple	33	en.wikipedia.org	Free for commercial use
32.	Borobudur Temple	33	Shutterstock	657962044
33.	Ishibutai Kofun	34	commons.wikimedia.com	Free for commercial use
34.	Ishi-no-Hoden	35	commons.wikipedia.com	Free for commercial use
35.	Masuda-no-Iwa	35	commons.wikipedia.com	Free for commercial use
36.	Utsuro Bune	36	www.rodrigoenok.blog.br	Free for commercial use
37.	Human Evolution Chart	37	animalia-life.club	Free for commercial use
38.	Yellow Emperor, Huangdi	38	cda.worldhistory.wikidot.com	Free for commercial use
39.	Chenrezig	39	www.flickr.com	Free for commercial use
40.	Lolladoff Plate	39	coolinterestingstuff.com	Free for commercial use
41.	Xianyang Pyramid	40	jackbrummet.blogspot	Free for commercial use
42.	Ancient Chinese/Alien War	40	www.flickr.com	Free for commercial use
43.	Red Headed Giants	41	modji-33.deviantart.com	Free for commercial use
44.	Great Wall of China	41	Shutterstock	93984988
45.	Chief Powhatan	42	www.pinterest.com	Free for commercial use
46.	Chichen Itza El Castillo	44	Shutterstock	161210453
47.	Calakmul	45	Shutterstock	441441046
48.	Teotihuacan	45	Shutterstock	181242512
49.	Feathered Serpent	46	commons.wikimedia.com	Free for commercial use
50.	Avenue of the Dead	46	Shutterstock	7667422

51.	Tenochtitlan	47	en.wikipedia.org	Free for comercial use
52.	Pyramid of the Magician	47	Shutterstock	578876149
53.	Palenque	48	Shutterstock	1009257328
54.	Pakal	48	My Picture	Free for commercial use
55.	Atlantean Figures	49	Shutterstock	197663540
56.	Tikal	49	Shutterstock	1041869116
57.	Caracol	50	Shutterstock	1026839890
58.	Xunantunich Belize	50	Shutterstock	496333753
59.	Montezuma II and Cortez	51	www.aoc.gov	Free for commercial use
60.	Pyramid Lake Petroglyphs	52	www.flickr.com	Free for commercial use
61.	Human Migration Patterns	52	commons.wikimedia.com	Free for commercial use
62.	Coral Castle	53	Pixabay	Free for commercial use
63.	Mesa Verde	53	Shutterstock	211847398
64.	Lost City of Atlantis	54	opsianic.blog.hr	Free for commercial use
65.	Merlin	55	Pixabay	Free for commercial use
66.	Odin	57	Shutterstock	491981284
67.	Hy-Brasil	57	aumagic.blogspot.com	Free for commercial use
68.	Crop Circles	58	groundreport/flickr/scagli	Free for commercial use
69.	Stonehenge	59	Shutterstock	81507649
70.	Tuatha De Danann	59	en.wikipedia.org	Free for commercial use
71.	Woodcuts in 1566	60	commons.wikimedia.org	Free for commercial use
72.	Jelling Stones	60	da.wikipedia.org/commons	Free for commercial use
73.	Asgard	61	scifi.stackexchange.com	Free for commercial use
74.	King Lalibela	63	www,flickr.com/commons.wiki	Free for commercial use
75.	Lalibela Churches	63	Shutterstock	504665104/152139971/430047499
76.	Ark of the Covenant	64	www.flickr.com	Free for commercial use
77.	Olmec Head	65	commons.wikimedia.org	Free for commercial use
78.	Ulama ball court	66	www.flickr.com	Free for commercial use
79.	Dogon Village	67	Shutterstock	90065443
80.	Nommo	67	Shutterstock	683244289
81.	Igigi	69	gity-novin.blogspot.com	Free for commercial use
82.	Anu	69	www.teinteresasaber.com	Free for commercial use
83.	Moses	70	Shutterstock	97358684
84.	Shroud of Turin	72	commons.wikimedia.org	Free for commercial use
85.	Siddhartha Gautama	73	Pixabay	Free for commercial use
86.	Maha Maya	74	en.wikipedia.org	Free for commercial use
87.	Vishnu	74	Pixabay	Free for commercial use
88.	Brahma/Shiva	74	lotussculpture/www.flickr.com	Free for commercial use
89.	Kailasa Temple	75	Shutterstock	472363555
90.	Ramayana	76	philosophicalanthropology	Free for commercial use
91.	Rama Setu	76	en.wikipedia.com	Free for commercial use
92.	Angkor Wat	77	Shutterstock/Pixabay	672858802 Free for com
93.	Vimana	78	magickriver.org	Free for commercial use
94.	Mahabharata	78	hif.wikipedia.org	Free for commercial use
95.	Zoroaster/Ahura Mazda	79	pluralism.com	Free for commercial use
96.	Gobekli Tepe	81	Shutterstock	643505296
97.	Nemrut Dagi	81	Shutterstock	1123377170
98.	Haunebu	82	discaircraft.greyfalcon.us	Free for commercial use
99.	Karahunj Observatory	83	www.flikr.com	Free for commercial use
100.	Celestial Greys	83	www.rodrigoenok.blog.br	Free for commercial use
101.	Viracocha	85	commons.wikipedia.org	Free for commercial use
102.	Puma Punku	86	cmns.wiki/themysteryvault.com	Free for commercial use
103.	Carel, Peru	87	pinterest.com	Free for commercial use
104.	Easter Island	87	Pixabay	Free for commercial use
105.	Copan	88	snipview.com/blacklistednews.	Free for commercial use
106.	K'inich Yax K'uk' Mo'	89	en.wikipedia.org	Free for commercial use

ABOUT THE AUTHOR

Michael Andre McCoy was born in Fort Lee, Virginia, and raised in the San Fernando Valley, a suburb of Los Angeles, California.

He attended Wayne State University in Detroit, Michigan, for two years on a track scholarship, majoring in Political Science and minoring in Psychology.

Upon returning to Southern California, he resumed his stage performances of original poetry and musical compositions, as well as attending the California State University at Northridge as a Philosophy major.

Michael graduated with honors from Morehouse College in Atlanta, Georgia, with a BA in Philosophy and a minor in Music.

Other books by Michaelandre McCoy

The Antitruth

The *MEAN*ing of America

Being Free

Schism (The Antitruth part 3)

The Me That Used To Be

The Keys To Haeven (The Antitruth part 4)

Banished From Haeven (The Antitruth part 5)

CPSIA information can be obtained
at www.ICGtesting.com
Printed in the USA
BVHW022116080919
557877BV00014B/484/P